NEMESIS

BLOOD TRAILS

Jermaine Rivers

Outskirts Press, Inc.
Denver, Colorado

Nemesis
Blood Trails

Outskirts Press
http://www.outskirtspress.com

ISBN-10: 1-59800-244-9
ISBN-13: 978-1-59800-244-7

Outskirts Press and the "OP" logo are trademarks belonging to
Outskirts Press, Inc.

Printed in the United States of America

Dedication

My Foundation

I dedicate this book to my parents Jerry and Brenda Rivers. All of my life you've provided me with the tools to be successful. Through the examples you set you taught me the importance of humility, charity and the power of prayer. Thank you for showing me what right looks like.

My Daughter

To my loving daughter Jovanni Rivers, you are my inspiration and motivating force. You are my legacy; all that I have in this world is yours. Your success in life will be determined by the sacrifices and decisions you make. We are all bound by our own imagination... if you think it you can achieve it. In your eyes I see infinite possibilities, let no one attempt to hinder your progress by setting your limitations.

Angles on the Battlefield

My Prayers go out to the men and women of the Armed Forces serving abroad; and to the families of those who made the ultimate sacrifice supporting Operation's Enduring and Iraqi Freedom.

"What we do in service of this great Nation has relevance."

Victory Start's Here

Prologue

I am the Archangel Raziel, an immortal, unchangeable and unaffected by the inevitabilities of time. I am a being of light, moving through a world of shadows, ever vigilant as I seek out those who fell from grace. Shortly after the creation of the universe, a battle was waged in Heaven that led to the earth realm. Angelic warriors were sent forth by Michael, bound by an unbreakable oath to eradicate all evil from the earth. I was among the legions empowered by the Creator to carry out this righteous task.

Many of my brothers fell in battle. Some were inexorably consumed by doubt and chose to forsake their oaths. Others were deceived by illusions, their minds slowly twisted over the ages, until they too fell into darkness. There are few of us who possess the strength to endure this daunting task. Nevertheless, we have spread out across the earth continuing our eternal search for the damned. Endlessly, I hunt those who seek to bring about the destruction of mankind.

There are some among you conscious enough to sense our presence in this world. Even greater are the number who refuse to believe my kind exists. I am powerful beyond measure, yet alone, and will remain so until my task is complete. Only after the last of those who fell from grace are returned to the dark realm may I re-enter the Gates of Heaven. Here is my journal, be not blinded by what you see, nor fooled by what you hear. Even now this battle is being waged around you, and the fate of all lie in the balance. Be warned, the fallen are among you…So am I.

CHAPTER 1
Reflections

Vanity and envy...two of the high sins which led to the inevitable downfall of many. That is the focal point of this eternal conflict and where my story begins. It all seems like a dream to me as I close my eyes and see things as they once were. There was once a time when harmony existed among my kind. That time has passed away from all except memory and shall never return. Vanity led the most powerful of us into darkness, and envy consumed the spirits of many who chose to follow in his path.

At first, my blind devotion did not allow me to understand the reasons why some of us began to stray from the path of obedience. Before the great battle which divided us occurred, I once heard tale of those who ventured secretly to the mortal realm and embellished themselves with earthly pleasures. These were the reckless immortals who took on human form and experienced the forbidden pleasures of the flesh.

Nothing had been gained from their actions except for attaining firsthand knowledge of sin and expulsion from heaven. Throughout the centuries of living amongst your kind I've come to realize certain undeniable truths. The most obvious is that we are all bound by our limitations; whether higher or lesser being, we are all creatures fashioned by god's infinite power and thereby are subject to his will.

You may be asking yourself right now, "Where is he going with all of this?" Well it is simple. What I give to you now, I offer freely. In a literal sense I'm placing in your hands the keys of understanding which will unlock the barriers of your mind; and give you clarity to the enigma which has eluded mankind for thousands of years. I'm not asking you to cast aside any of the metaphysical, or theological beliefs that you may have grown to accept. I am well aware that humans tend to believe only those things which appeal to them the most.

For those of you who are not mentally reclusive, I offer you the chance to look into the portals of my mind and see things as they once were. Before I proceed with my tale, the general rules must be honored—as with all things that are extended to mortals it can only be given if you accept it with your free will. I can not force this vision upon you...but should you accept my gift, you shall be taken on a spiritual journey across the barriers of time and space; back to the very place where the struggle between good and evil began.

This journey is not intended for the faint of heart, those who accept my offer will possess an awareness of the world as never before. You will no longer be a part of the general populace who go about life in a spiritually vegetated state. If you were to look about your surroundings right now, chances are you may be able to identify one of the hapless individuals of whom I speak.

In this age of man it is not hard to pick out the loud and obnoxious person from a crowd. One who is bereft of all moral fiber and inhibition; the self absorbed creature who cares nothing for the world around them, indulging their every whim...usually at someone else's expense. Then you have those who live without faith, believing that all of their good fortunes are a result of their own doing. Not recognizing the dark forces that pit their will against them. Many of you may find truth in what I say, yet there will be those who are naturally skeptical to all things they never had to experience personally. To the skeptics I say this: Should you ever find yourself being robbed by a man at gun point, understand that even though your assailant may have his finger on the trigger, it is often a physical manifestation of pure evil lurking in some dark corner close by, watching the whole spectacle unfold with a grin on his face. In essence this is the very nature of the beings that I hunt...they are the unseen voices that whisper in the ear of the criminal minded, encouraging them to cast aside morality and pull the trigger. Acts of desperation always seem to carry grave consequences. My role has always been to urge those desperate and misguided individuals to reconsider the destructive path they have chosen. Every now and then I find myself having to take a more hands on approach with those who are too far gone to see the danger of their lifestyles.

Far too long and with painful eyes I've watched the seeds of hatred grow and corrupt the human heart. Throughout the ages of man, from the birth of one civilization to the destruction of another your kind has been caught in the center of a struggle between good and evil. I am one of the few who chose to stay on earth and protect humanity against those who seek to prevent your kind from reaching the potential it is destined to achieve.

Even I cannot imagine all of the possibilities that you have...make no mistake of it, because of the indigenous human ability to reason and grow spiritually, a large bounty has been placed upon every last one of your souls. That is of course why we are here right now. It is because of the fear of one cosmic entity becoming insubstantial next to a seemingly inferior being who has been fashioned in the likeness of our creator who has no limit and no conceivable bounds. Imagine the infinite possibilities of the creature which is man — please forgive me, I sometimes become overwhelmed by my own thoughts and tend to rant, believe me its been awhile since I allowed myself the luxury of making my personal thoughts known to anyone. Its quite possible that I could have went on with this lengthy monologue forever, unfortunately you would be no closer to understanding the truth than before you opened the pages of my journal. That in itself would do nothing more than defeat my purpose entirely. I know that time is very precious to mortals, and with that in mind I will be brief and hopefully not bore you with the incessant fillers of an immortal. If you are to understand the ways our enemy, you must surrender yourself to me completely, open your mind and see the world as it once was but through my eyes. Go back with me to the beginning of this struggle where a third of heaven led by Lucifer rose up against our creator and in their defeat fell from grace.

The Great Battle

Infinite seemed the number of Lucifer's demons that filled the Heavens. My senses were bombarded by the presence of the unholy, as they were cast out of heaven consumed in flames. Their screams and pleas for mercy went out in vain as I slashed through demonic flesh and Michael, commander of the Heavenly legions, unleashed the wrath of God.

As I gazed towards the great light, I saw five of my angelic brothers beginning their ascent towards the sacred throne of Heaven. All of creation was brought forth to bear witness. I watched Michael as he approached the apex of heaven and take up his station: never before had his gaze looked so fierce. Armed with both his shield and sword, Michael was in full battle dress. Among our number, he was seen as the most perfect warrior, created from the most resilient elements of the cosmos.

His purpose above all others was to defend the throne of God and lead the legions of Heaven into battle should ever the need arise. Now as he stood looking out over us, there were no songs of praises being sung in Heaven, only an emptiness which hung in the air. At the base of the throne, I saw three beings quaking in fear, brought to their knees in total submission. Michael stood poised behind them with his right hand resting upon the hilt of his sword, his armored breastplate of silver and gold beamed with the light of divinity. Long silver colored hair flowed freely across his back.

Massive wings of white and gold streaked feathers were folded serenely behind his back. His face was devoid of emotion, and his steel gaze was focused on the beings in his custody. To the right of Michael stood the Archangel Gabriel the messenger of God.

Slung across Gabriel's back was a massive horn of ivory trimmed in gold. I looked towards the base of the throne at the three beings who knelt face down against the floor. Their transgressions were unknown to me, yet it was clear that one would soon judge them.

As I looked closer, I began to notice that the three angelic captives had altered their forms to mimic that of mortals. Despite their skills of deception, two of them were unable to successfully duplicate human form. In each of them I found obvious flaws to their shameful manifestations. One being had unnaturally elongated arms and legs, totally unlike natural human proportions. The other being was the exact opposite of the first, possessing a more squat and compact body, with short, stocky legs.

In the midst of the three captives was Lucifer. It came as no surprise to see that he had taken on the guise of Adam. Despite how perfect this image seemed, I saw clearly through his blasphemous disguise. Never before in our existence had an immortal attempted this, mainly because the necessity to do so was never there. All of our angelic functions never required direct interaction with humanity, and the act of intervention was forbidden. Yet here was Lucifer, in all his arrogance, taking on this form.

Though he was brought to his knees, he showed neither fear nor remorse. I knew him well. His pride would not abide the notion of showing fear; he wanted everyone present to see his audacity and this act of defiance. Gabriel took the massive horn from his back. Lifting it up to his lips, he blew one long continuous note which shook the foundations of Heaven. At that exact moment, I could feel a massive source of power begin to shift as it surged throughout the universe. It was as though every particle in the air was being concentrated into one place.

All who were in attendance fell silent. Only the faintest rustling of wings could be heard across the entire realm. Intangible particles surged and crackled as an immense life force pulsated and flowed through us in continuous waves. The entire universe shifted as the presence of God began to manifest before the heavenly assemblage. Immediately the two angels that were next to Lucifer quaked with fear.

Gabriel let forth another loud blast from his horn then surveyed the masses, accounting for each and every being that should be in attendance. After he was satisfied that no one was overlooked, Gabriel withdrew and took up his place next to Michael. All that were present bowed in unison, showing reverence to the king of Creation. A moment of silence passed, and then God spoke.

"Among you are those guilty of disobeying my divine law. In secret places some have whispered treasonous words against me, challenging all of the goodness which I have wrought. Am I not the supreme sovereign who presides here and in all other places? Was it not I that created everything before you and declared it to be both perfect and good? All of these wonders I have brought into existence, yet there are some of you who are discontented and seek to go against me."

His focus was now upon the three beings that kneeled before him. In a booming voice, he addressed one of the beings directly, calling it by name.

"Lucifer, the time of reckoning is at hand and repentance is your only chance for redemption. Tell me the places you've been and the works you have set into motion. Speak to me only that which is true, for you above all know I am not one to be deceived."

"I have done only that which you have instructed me to do," Lucifer replied in a stern voice. "For so long have I obeyed your laws and watched over your creations, I have no other purpose than to do your bidding and entertain your every whim.

"Is my devotion to serve you not clear? If you would but look upon me with favorable eyes as you once did you could see truth in me. Even now, I bear resemblance to your beloved Adam, hoping to receive for myself a trace of the affinity you have for him. I am the only true servant you have. No one here has gone to such lengths to assist you in creating perfection. Yet here I stand before you accused of wrongdoings."

"Do not attempt to beguile me with your tantalizing yet deceitful words," God said angered by Lucifer's word play.

"I am not so easily moved by your colorful rhetoric; however, I am more interested in your recent ventures to the mortal plane."

"During my travels to the mortal plane, I have seen many of the wonders that you've created," Lucifer replied. "Unfortunately, like myself, others who watched as I did have noticed flaws in some of the things you've created."

There was a great commotion in heaven among all who heard these words. After hearing Lucifer refer to the creator's work as flawed, many of my brothers went into a state of unrest. Thunder echoed across the heavens, and the command for silence was given.

"Lucifer, tell me about the flaws that you and those like you have found. Tell me of these imperfections which you claim to have found in the world that I have created."

Lucifer began to rise slowly to his feet until he stood erect. An air of boldness radiated all around him. His head was held high with pride, and his eyes strained as he attempted to look directly into the radiant light which engulfed us all.

"Lord, during my journey to the earth realm, I observed many wondrous things indeed. I swam the oceans and seas you created and took note of the endless variety of creatures which inhabit the waters. All that I saw seemed to prosper and thrive by developing a natural equilibrium with their environment.

"Even the trees and other vegetation of the earth seem to grow together in unison, establishing a sense of harmony. No doubt all of this is a direct credit to your enormous grace," Lucifer said sarcastically as he lowered his head. "As I and, dare I forget, those like me as you put it, continued our vigilance, it became evident that all your creations seemed to be nothing more than weak and unsubstantial creatures, creatures that struggle day after day for survival, only to perish after you turn your glance away from them.

"Why should anything created by you be made to suffer? Everything I've seen on the mortal plane is consistent with my theory and seems to share the same cruel fate. It seems that each of your creations are given a glimmer of hope, only to be cut down by the cold touch of oblivion. Not one of them can endure what we do, and I find it absolutely boring to just merely watch them as you would have me do.

"Tell me, Father, are my brothers and I destined to share this same fate? Have you only extended our existence in this universe solely for your personal enjoyment? Or will there come a time when you tire of us too, and have us perish like the lilies of the field when winter comes? Answer me, oh Great Father, do you really have a plan for any of us, or is our presence so uninviting and unendurable that in your boredom you choose to push us away. Is this what we are meant to do for all eternity?"

Lucifer's statement caused another great commotion to rise among the angelic assemblage. Throughout the heavens questions began to rise, which began to spread doubt among the ranks like wildfire. Randomly, the once devoted and faithful began to turn towards one another to question the things he just mentioned.

Lucifer continued to build his momentum by saying, "The fish in the seas last less than a season and the flowers of the field cannot withstand the cold winters. All of these things you in your wisdom set into motion. Last but not least, there is your beloved man. Of all your wondrous creations, mankind, in my eyes, is ranked the weakest and most pathetic of all. I've looked into the future of you beloved creation and all I see is a perverted race of beings who has already disregarded the grace you have extended them.

Like it or not humanity is destined to fail…in time brother will turn against brother, and the world you created will be stained from the blood of the battles they will fight. Even now they are at to war with one another. They place their love for silver and gold above one another… to include you. Yet ironically, it is mankind whom you love above us all."

Heaven shook with the cries that came from the unfaithful angels that had been captivated by Lucifer's every word.

There was a smug look of satisfaction on his face; knowing that he had set the inevitable wheels of chaos into motion, Lucifer turned his back on the presence of god and looked down at those who had bought into his web of lies. The Lord's command for silence brought an end to the boisterous commotion. After regaining order, he continued to speak.

"For all of your cunning and beguiling rhetoric, you understand nothing. It's obvious that you forget yourself, and in doing so your arrogance has led you to make an even greater error. You have forgotten who I am as well I am the source from which all things flow. Nothing could have been or would be if not for me. I am the grand architect who has set all that is into motion.

"I am perfect, blameless, and completely without error. I do not know the meaning of flaws because I am without mistake. All that you have witnessed is a part of my plan, and that is something far beyond any lesser being to ponder—especially one such as you."

The thin thread of control that once held Lucifer at bay had been severed. His entire body began to tremble in anger as he raised a fist towards the overwhelming presence before him and said, "Lesser being, you say? I'm the one who has been running behind you fixing everything that you have bungled throughout time. You shall regret those words…I will take with me those who are not blinded by your flaws and I will re-create the world in my image! "

After hearing Lucifer's challenging words, a countless number of the unfaithful that were in our midst spread their wings and lifted their voices to praise Lucifer, proclaiming him as their new lord. Aroused by his act of defiance, they lifted their swords and shields in the air and proceeded to bang metal upon metal, causing a horrible clanging noise, one which had never been heard in heaven before.

I pressed my hands against my ears, attempting to lessen the impact of the noise around me. There was still a large number of the faithful present. Our devotion to the

Father had not wavered as we listened to Lucifer weave his web of lies.

Angered by the insolent reactions of those whom Lucifer had won over, God in all his fury cursed them all and said, "Those of you who in heart and spirit wish to join Lucifer, I cast you out. You will be condemned to dwell in the bottomless pit of hell along side your master for all eternity. Rule in hell, Lucifer, among your demonic horde, for Heaven and all that I have created shall never be yours to taint or destroy.

With the lord's decree, I saw a third of the host of Heaven transformed into hideous creatures. Reptilian countenances replaced the beautiful angelic beings that once sang praises to our master. Now their wretched mouths uttered foul and profane curses upon him. Those of us who were loyal were spared the torment suffered by the unfaithful. We gathered together, forming a wall of steel around the throne of the Father. One by one, Lucifer's minions made their assaults.

One after another, they came down upon us in a flood of rage. Michael and I stood back to back, sword and shield in hand, holding Lucifer's demonic hordes at bay. Thousands of the faithful came to our aid, fighting alongside us without compassion or regard for the damned. Fiercely, we battled against overwhelming odds until we managed to push a large number of Lucifer's demons away from the base of the throne and beyond the towering pillars of gold that lined the walls of the immense chamber.

Infinite seemed the number of Lucifer's demons that filled the Heavens. My senses were bombarded by the presence of the unholy, as they swooped down upon us from above, only to be cut down and cast out of Heaven, consumed in flames. Their screams and pleas for mercy went out in vain as I slashed through their demonic flesh. For each one that fell beneath our combined might, another demon sprang up in its place, until the sky was darkened by the dark lord's winged minions.

We managed to force the battle out of the massive gates. Once outside the threshold of Heaven, Gabriel let forth two powerful blasts from his horn. It was as if an invisible hand had closed the towering gates behind us. With a thunderous clamor the entrance to heaven was closed barring all to enter the regions within.

Once outside the golden realm, we reorganized our numbers. It was clear that the tide of the battle had shifted in our favor. With each stroke of our swords, we sent the demons plummeting down towards the earth, engulfed in flames. I do not know how long we fought; it seemed as though time itself stood still.

Michael had fought his way through thousands of Lucifer's underlings in search of their master. None could withstand the sheer explosive power of his blows; his expertise in wielding steel was second to none. Whether in flight or on the ground, no foe proved to be a match for him. Each of his movements were fluid as his weapon zinged through the air. No matter what direction the assault came from, Michael parried to block one attack, only to follow up with a series of slash combinations of his own.

Shields were shattered and limbs were rendered to smoldering ash as his weapon found its mark. Michael remained relentless as he faced thousands of attackers that tried to keep him from their cowering master who receded deeper into their ranks.

I took to the air and joined Michael as we fought through one wave of winged demons after another, pursuing Lucifer across the heavens, rendering his demonic horde to ash with each stroke of our flaming swords.

It wasn't long before our pursuit came to a close and we stood face to face with the dark lord. He beat his ebony wings against the air forcefully and hovered in the air thousands of feet above the earth. Only a few of his closest henchmen circled around him in a ring of death, while below us the numbers of his minions were being reduced to nothing. Defiant to the end, Lucifer taunted us with his words, all the while his sword dripped with the blood of our comrades.

"You fools, this was to be my time to ascend to power." Lucifer said in a heated tone. Since the dawn of time I have planned for this day but you self-righteous idiots have ruined it all. In an effort to save himself .Lucifer looked at Raziel and extended his hand towards him and said, "I sense doubt in you Raziel...you know there is truth in what I say, yet you continue to serve him. Take my hand and swear allegiance to me as your sovereign, the reward for your obedience shall be great. I shall extend this offer to you only once."

"I always knew that vanity would be your undoing. Raziel said. Save your offer Lucifer we both know that they are nothing more than empty promises that will never be fulfilled. Nothing you possess could ever turn me from the path of righteousness."

"I have no time to waste on fledglings such as you. Come let us bring this chase to an end." Lucifer said in a tone filled with hatred.

Poised for battle, I started to focus my energies for what would be the greatest opponent I had ever faced. I had no doubt that with our combined strength, Lucifer could be vanquished. Before I could lunge forward into battle, I felt Michael's strong hand on my arm holding me fast. Puzzled by his hesitation, I turned to look at him, and he shook his head.

"No Raziel, powerful as you may be, you are not ready to do battle with the likes of him. Lucifer and I have always known that the day would come where our mettle would be tested in combat. I was created specifically for this moment. On my mark, you take out his minions, but leave Lucifer to me. Michael stared directly into my eyes, and only after I nodded my head in acknowledgement did he loosen the steel-like grip he had on me.

We both turned to see Lucifer grinning and licking his lips as though he had been overtaken by a blood lust. His henchmen continued their rotations around him, beckoning either one of us into their death trap.

Michael beat his wings against the air and in a streak of light dived towards his enemy. A surge of courage seemed to well up and explode inside of Lucifer as he charged forward in flight to meet Michael head-on in battle. No words can truly describe the sheer concussive impact that was made when the two irresistible forces collided. The shock waves produced when Lucifer and Michael exchanged blows rocked the foundations of the earth. Back and forth they fought across the heavens, and despite Lucifer's physical prowess, Michael proved to be the more powerful of the two when it came to sheer brute strength. Each of his blows connected with explosive force.

It wasn't long before Michael had sent the leader of the demon horde flailing towards the earth like a blazing comet. The impact of Lucifer's fall was so tremendous that a crater three kilometers in diameter was left in its wake. Though the fallen Angel lay in the crater on the verge of defeat, he still refused to yield.

Many of my brothers sought to take advantage of his momentary weakness and closed in around him. Defiant to the end, Lucifer continued to strike out at those who encased him within a mountain of steel. Despite our overpowering number, we proved inferior to Lucifer's strength. Hundreds perished beneath his blows. It wasn't long until the last of his forces had regrouped and formed a perimeter around their master.

While thousands of angelic warriors continued their frontal assault on the demonic horde, Michael and I took a legion of archangels to flank the last of Lucifer's minions who came to the aid of their master. One by one, Michael and I dispatched them until we penetrated the wall of fallen angels that surrounded our adversary. Swiftly, Michael bore down upon Lucifer, grasping him by the throat and squeezed with all his might until his foe sank to his knees in submission.

Then Michael raised his flaming sword high into the air and plunged it deeply into Lucifer's chest. The dark lord screeched in agony as a portion of his heavenly powers were slowly absorbed into the weapon. Stripped of his divinity, he was now weakened to the point where he was no longer a threat. Lucifer now lay motionless against the earth, defeated.

From the gaping wound in his chest flowed the darkest and most fowl liquid. It spread out like a luminous shadow, and anything it touched withered and died.

As it continued to spread, we all stepped clear of its poisonous touch. Michael alone had the power to rid the world of this threat. Raising his sword towards Heaven, he began to speak the sacred rites in the ancient tongue, invoking aid from the supreme being. Slowly his weapon began to glow until it blazed with a light more brilliant than that of the sun.

In one swift motion he stabbed deep into the earth, causing it to shift and open into a great crevice revealing a dimensional portal of a place far removed from the mortal plane.

Flames danced up from the fissure and poisonous gasses seeped out from the gaping crack. Into the fiery chasm Michael flung his once proud and boastful adversary along with any demon who lay about. All that were present took up the task of pursuing the elusive demons who had witnessed the fall of their master yet chose to flee. God's will had been done as the cursed were being cast into the bottomless pit. Michael stood above the fissure and made his solemn proclamation.

"Hear me. Lucifer is henceforth banished from heaven. By God's will he has been stripped of his divine power and grace. Let his name go unspoken in our halls and the light of the morning star be erased from the constellation." In one fluid motion, Michael stabbed deeply into the earth and twisted his sword as though it were a great key. The ground shook beneath our feet as the gates of hell began to close, imprisoning the fallen angel and his minions for all time. It seemed as though the battle had been won and that we were victorious. Then, from Earth we could hear the great horn of Gabriel sound out, beckoning for us to return home. Light pierced the dark clouds that had once covered the earth and heavenly light shown through. Those of us who battled and tracked our demonic prey ceased our hunt, knowing that we were being summoned home.

Swifter than the speed of light, we took flight towards the gates of Heaven. Our weapons were stained from the blood of our enemies. Michael was the first to land before the towering gates. He wasted little time as he approached Gabriel, saying, "Why have you summoned us back to the sacred threshold? This battle is far from over. I have imprisoned Lucifer, yet his forces even now are fleeing across the four corners of the earth attempting to regroup."

"I am aware of all that you say," Gabriel replied. "Yet within these very walls a battle is being waged by a formidable number of the fallen who are intent upon overthrowing the Kingdom of Heaven. You must decide who shall remain here to fight and who shall return to the earth realm to pursue the last remnants of Lucifer's demonic horde who will eventually make attempts at freeing their master. They will not rest until he is released to exact his vengeance upon us."

Turning towards his band of battle fatigued warriors, Michael thrust out his sword and said, "Who among you shall take on the task of pursuing the remaining demonic horde on the mortal plane? Time is of the essence and you must decide now, even though seconds pass in this realm, decades are being allotted to the forces of evil who flee into the darker regions of the earth seeking to replenish their numbers."

I was among the first warriors to step forward and accept this task. We each took an oath never to reenter the heavenly gates until every demon on earth had been found and cast into hell. Once on earth, each of us assumed human form and went our separate ways in search for the damned, still bound by the original decree of not interfering with humanity as we proceeded with our seemingly endless hunt.

Mine is an existence of isolation and never-ending conflict. No matter the odds, I shall not deviate from the path that I have chosen until my task is complete. There is an enemy who does not rest and constantly plots the downfall of mankind. Slowly he is re-gaining his strength, using the souls of hapless mortals who have pledged their life to his dark cause. Be not fooled by what you hear, nor blinded by what you see. There is an ancient war being waged on earth, and the fate of the world lies in the balance. Be warned, the fallen are among you, and so am I.

CHAPTER 2

Blood Trials

A man sit's patiently in the passenger seat of a dimly lit vehicle. He presses a button on his timepiece and the digital numbers on his watch come to life. It was now 11:30 p.m., and his patrol of the city was almost over. Officer John Graham was an average, everyday beat cop from the 32nd Precinct based in downtown Jersey City. Being a seasoned vet with eighteen years on the force, he had seen many things that tested his faith and resolve. Until now he thought he'd seen it all. Nothing in all his years of training and experience could possibly have prepared him for this.

"Rain, rain, and more rain! Seven days of this crap and it still ain't letting up," said Cadet Baker as he wiped furiously at the mist which had collected on the inside of the squad car's windshield. Across from him in the passenger seat sat Officer John Graham, a senior observer and evaluator who looked over at him and shook his head in disbelief of what he was witnessing. For the last ten minutes Graham watched as the young, frustrated rookie wiped incessantly at the windows around him.

John began to wonder how long the kid could keep up this routine. "No one can be this stupid," he thought to himself. After having his fill of the spectacle, John slowly reached over and flipped a switch on the console. Immediately a gush of cool air flowed out of the vents. Within moments, the windows were clear, and the metropolitan scenery outside was no longer a blur. The seasoned officer didn't have to say a word. Instead, he leaned back nonchalantly in his seat as the young man assigned to him turned red with embarrassment. The city around them appeared to come to life as they passed down the lightly trafficked avenue. Pedestrians walked along the sidewalks shielded by their umbrellas; some even attempted to find cover from the rain beneath the ledges of department stores. Although the fog within the vehicle had passed, the mood was clearly too tense for even John to handle. Looking over at the frustrated and now embarrassed trainee, John said. "Lighten up a little, kid. If you grip the steering wheel any tighter, you're going to break the damn thing!"

"Sorry sir. "Cadet Baker replied. I need this evaluation to graduate. I came too far to get booted out of the Academy now." Baker eased back away from the wheel and took a deep breath. "I can't help it. I've always been a perfectionist; I get it from my Pop. "Continue to raise the bar…don't settle for second best," he always said. He was a cop too, you know. He died on the job when I was seventeen. My mom wanted me to do something safe, like becoming an accountant or something like that. I wanted to follow in my dad's footsteps. I can't help it, I guess, three generations of police officers It's in my blood."

The young man's pale knuckles slowly started to regain their color once he loosened his death grip on the steering wheel.

"Take it easy, top cop; you'll do just fine," John said. "First thing you need to learn is how not to sweat the small stuff! Besides, the defroster is busted; sometimes it works, sometimes it doesn't. Next time just crack your window and the problem will eventually fix itself."

"*I didn't realize they let guys into the academy so young?*"—— *What the hell am I talking about, I was the same age too when I signed up.*" John thought to himself as he looked over at the inexperienced cadet. Police Cadet Raymond

Baker was twenty-one years old, practically still a kid, plucked fresh from the bosom of safety. All the training he received on law enforcement came in the form of situational exercises and class room lectures on criminal psychology. Since our shift began Baker shifted from side to side in the driver's seat trying to get comfortable, the only time he seemed to be at ease was when he was pulling people over and handing out citations. Every now and then he would say something witty in an attempt to gain my approval. I stopped counting after the tenth citation he gave for driver's who failed to come to complete stops at intersections. I practically had to stop him from going berserk on an old lady he pulled over for changing lanes without using her turn signals.

"Don't be in such a rush to make a name for yourself kid... if you make it past me, this very well may be the part of town that you get assigned to." John said as he jotted down a few notes on the clipboard he carried. You gotta learn how to establish a rapport with the locals before you start bustin their chop's. Look around you... some of the people that you see have been working and living in this district their entire lives. Get to know them, earn their respect and gain their trust."

"Besides, no one likes a hard ass... only rookies hand out citations for minor infraction like those." The cadet kept an watchful eye on the road but nodded his head in acknowledgement. He knew that he just received some good advice from a veteran who's been around for a while. "The kid is wound up a little tight for his own good, but for the most part I think he'll do fine — that is if he learn to pace himself and don't get burned out.

Overall John had the feeling that the young man who sat next to him intentions were in the right place. During their time together Baker didn't say or do anything which lead him to believe otherwise. Over the years he'd seen his fair share of loose cannons, and on rare occasions crooked cop's, who got caught up accepting bribes from local drug dealers. In every class there's always one who slip through the cracks, but like every other cadet that he had trained there was always the ones like Raymond Baker; a second generation police officer who tried to make a good impression. It really didn't matter that they guy had the jitters... he had a right to be nervous, after all he was being evaluated on his performance and John remembered how squeamish he was on his first patrol.

A lot of things had changed since he was a cadet at the police academy. Eighteen years had passed since he first took the oath to serve and protect. John pulled down the sun visor and looked at his reflection in the mirror. He just celebrated his thirty-ninth birthday and with all of the abuse his body had taken over the years, he felt every bit of his age. At the moment, all he could think of was getting off duty, taking a hot shower and getting some sleep. He felt exhausted and looked a mess, in this line of work those were two bad combinations. All of the long nights and early mornings working these streets have finally caught up to him, John thought to himself.

Placing a hand upon his chin he turned his head slightly from side to side examining his scruffy profile. "I definitely need to shave." John said as he scratched at the stubbles of his five o clock shadow. His deep blue eye's were intense, yet red with fatigue. His face had strong features, you cold tell with one glance that he was not afraid to get down and dirty if he had too. Being a cop for so long he was harden by his experiences.

All of the evidence was engraved within the deep contours of his face. John took note of the small wrinkles that had begun to set in at the corners of his eyes and around his mouth. His dark brown hair was beginning to thin at his hairline, for years he wore a high and tight, he always thought it made him look more intimidating. For the most part he was an intimidating figure. He stood over six feet and was two hundred and fifteen pounds of lean muscle. Not bad for a guy pushing forty, John thought as he closed the visor and looked down at his watch. "It's was quarter till midnight kid... lets call it a day. You'll receive the results of the examination tomorrow afternoon." John said as he closed the lid on his clipboard.

"If you don't mind me asking sir— how did I do?" Baker inquired in a low voice.

"You'll find out tomorrow kid, now turn this bucket around and get us back to the precinct ASAP." John replied as he tried to keep from smiling. He glanced over at the cadet again, and for a brief second almost saw himself. Baker looked like a younger version of him, except he was about twenty pounds lighter and had brown eyes. He even sported a high and tight hair cut similar to his.

At least he looked like a cop, but it will take some time before he'd stop smelling like fresh meat. To the untrained eye Baker might have seemed pretty convincing, but he wasn't official just yet. His uniform was pressed, and the leather utility belt he wore around his waist still smelled brand new. Despite the limited visibility from the rain Baker managed to find a side street to turn their vehicle around. As they made their way through the business district of downtown Jersey City, John looked on with intent eyes as people went about their lives despite the unfavorable weather conditions.

Each one seemed to be in their own world, as they walked carelessly around one another, trying to get out of the rain. He spotted a young woman leaving a convenience store with a bag of groceries cradled in each arm. A man who was walking with a cell phone pressed against his ear took no notice of her as she emerged from the store. Without breaking his stride he ran into her knocking the items out of her hands and all over the damp sidewalk. After the collision he looked back but keep going on about his business as though he didn't have a care in the world. No one else seemed to care to stop and offer her assistance as she struggled on her hands and knees to gather her belongings which had been strewn across the walkway.

How many times had he witnessed scenes like this? John wasn't surprised at this type of behavior. It was actually common to see citizens in large cities such as this to turn a blind eye to one another. Their squad car came to an abrupt halt as a street light above them turned red. A haggard, elderly woman in dirty and weather beaten clothing pushed an overflowing shopping cart filled with random articles across the street in front of them.

"That cart probably contains everything she owns in this world," John said. Baker had stopped wiping at the fog filled windshield momentarily to look over at the woman who crossed their path, then hunched his shoulders in a dismissive fashion and continued to clear his view of the mist. John continued to watch the woman as she stopped only to rummage through restaurant dumpsters in search her next meal.

John shook his head and looked down at his watch again it was midnight and their shift was officially over. "A few more minutes and I'm home free—hot shower here I come." John said to himself. When he looked up again, something he'd seen from an alley they had passed caught his attention.

"Whoa, Baker, slow down. Did you see that?"

"See what?" the cadet replied. "I can't see nuthin through this damn rain!"

"Well I did, so turn around and head back down that alley we just passed."

Officer Graham flipped a switch on the console that activated the unit's floodlights and sirens. Through the pouring rain, John caught a glimpse of something that appeared to be a struggle. Within seconds, Baker had the squad car turned around and was moving down the trash-filled alley. Upon entering the alley, they saw the figure of a man crouched over a woman sprawled out in the middle of the street.

The squad car screeched to a halt about ten feet from the scene. Baker jumped out and moved into position. In one fluid motion he drew his weapon and had it aimed at the man who was crouched over the woman. The rain fell in thick sheets that pelted the cadet's face. Though he struggled to see through the rain, Baker could make out a thick steam of blood coming from the spot where the woman lay. Her purse and the contents within it were scattered along the ground. She was dressed in skimpy clothing that was far too revealing for her to have been associated with a professional occupation.

Judging by her red fishnet stockings and knee high boots, it didn't take a genius to see that the woman was a prostitute. The makeup which had been applied heavily around her eyes and lips had been smeared by the rain. All that was left of her mascara ran down the contours of her cheeks in two thin black streams. Her long red hair was completely drenched and covered half of her face. She had to have been in her mid twenties, but the lines that were embedded in her facial features gave her a more older and disheveled appearance.

Despite the rain which pelted her entire body the woman didn't move at all. Fearing the worst Baker assumed that she was probably dead. Despite her choice of employment she was still a human being, and no one should be left in this filth among the heaps of trash and refuse. The world around him seemed to move in slow motion, and the longer Baker watched her laying there the hotter his blood began to boil

As he looked close he could see that the woman's head was situated in an unnatural position, like her neck had been broken. From the way her eyes protruded from the sockets and her tongue dangled from her mouth she probably had been strangled as well. Whatever the cause of death might have been it was clear that she died in agony.

Baker had never seen this level of violence before, the fact that it had been inflicted upon this woman made him angry. Immediately he began to shout out orders to the man who slowly rose from a kneeling position to his full height. What stood before them was a young man seemingly no older than twenty-five years old. He was extremely well built, and even though both of the policemen stood over six foot, he towered above them both.

His long, silvery hair flowed down and across his shoulders. The man's hands were positioned down at his sides both palms facing out. He stood motionless as streams of water ran down into his face. The man didn't make any sudden movements; he stood absolutely still looking directly into Baker eyes, steadily holding his gaze.

John had also drawn his handgun and began to move into position. Keeping an eye on the suspect at all times he looked down at the body of the dead girl. Her throat had been cut, and her shirt was torn open, exposing a freshly-carved satanic pentagram that covered her entire chest.

"Step away from the body, interlace your fingers, place them on top of your head, and face the wall behind you." Officer Graham spoke with authority as he edged in closer with his 45-caliber handgun drawn and aimed at the suspect. The mysterious man continued to stand motionless, staring at Graham. Then he turned his glance back down at the girl. Graham was about ten feet from him now. Despite the rain coming down in sheets, he was close enough to get a good look at him. His eyes were radiant and had the appearance of metallic orbs. Theirs were a color John had never seen before, a mixture between silver and blue. From behind him John could hear Baker talking over the radio, giving their location and situation to the dispatcher, requesting for paramedics.

"Good!" John thought, "The kid had paid attention in class after all, calling in for back up, sticking to procedures!" Though he had serious doubt that the girl was alive, that was still the right thing to do in this situation. Within minutes there were going to be at least two more units on the scene to assist, whether needed or not. The prime objective at this point was to take this guy down and bring him in to the station for questioning.

After repeating the same orders twice, Officer Graham assumed that either he didn't understand English, or wasn't going down without a fight. John knew he was going to have to do this one by the numbers. After Baker had finished his call for backup they moved in towards the suspect with their weapons drawn. The man acted as though they were not even there, he stared off into the distance as though he was searching for something or someone. Baker was now within arms' reach of the man who was now looking past them.

Talking calmly to the suspect, he attempted to put a set of hand cuffs on one of the suspect's wrists. Graham knew he should have been the one to take the lead on this one but experience is probably the best teacher. So far the kid was doing all the right things, if the suspect were to get out of hand he'd be there to step in and take over. No sooner than he had assured himself of the rookie's grasp on the situation, Baker had gotten frustrated and loss control. because the man had not surrendered to being placed in the restraining device.

Drawing his nightstick, Baker decided to bring the brute down by striking him at the back of his knees. With his club raised high in the air it was clear that Cadet Baker was poised to strike. Before he could unleash his blow, something changed in the facial expression of the suspect who had allowed the inexperienced cadet to touch him. The man's entire demeanor shifted from that of a gentle giant to an animal who senses danger. It was as though Baker's movements were in slow motion, though he managed to swing his club he missed his target entirely. The man had turned around to face his assailant, then with one swift movement he shoved the young cadet and sent him sailing across the alley into a pile of trash cans fifty feet away. The impact rendered him unconscious instantly. That was enough to set Graham into action.

Aiming his weapon at the man's shoulder, he fired one single shot. A flash of silver streaked directly past him and down the alley, disappearing into the rain-filled night. Graham scanned the area checking the shadows making sure the area was clear. "No human moves that fast!" he said to himself. With his weapon drawn at the high ready, John began to walk backwards towards a nearby wall. From left to right he scanned the alley for traces of the mystery man. Trying to gather his wits, Graham made his way towards the unconscious cadet.

Suddenly, he heard a noise from above that sounded like the rustling of wings and garments which settled directly behind him. He turned around on his heels and swung his weapon up to head level preparing to take a shot. He stood face to face with the suspect who had reappeared out of thin air. Within less than a second the man had disarmed Officer Graham and held him in a steel-like grip. Their eyes were locked in a fierce gaze. Though his lips did not move John heard the man's a voice being projected into his mind.

"Why do you attempt to prosecute me?" I am one who has watched over your kind throughout the ages. Know this...I am not your enemy, but I seek the one who did this evil tonight. Weapons such as the ones you possess are useless against it as well as me. Do not pursue it, this foe is far beyond any of you." Even though the man held him captive, John felt no menace from him. As the mystery man projected his thoughts into Graham's mind, a comforting feeling came over him. The trance was broken by the sound of approaching sirens.

Quickly he turned around and focused his attention towards the opening of the alley. Gently he released Officer Graham and disappeared into the shadows. John slowly made his way towards the stunned cadet who was starting to regain consciousness. After recovering his gun which had been tossed among the debris he checked Baker for injuries and helped him to his feet.

"Ouch! Did you get the license plate number of the truck that ran my ass over? What the hell just happened?" Baker said rubbing the bruise that was forming on the back of his head.

"You got cocky and damn near got your ass killed, hot shot!" John replied

"Well, where is he at now? Please tell me you nailed him after he got me."

"He got away, but don't worry he won't get far ...I got a good look at him before he hauled ass" John said. Methodically, he began searching the alley for clues of what actually happened. He knew that their backup would be there at any moment, and that meant he would have to give a full report. " I guess that warm shower was gonna have to wait a few more hours. John said to himself. Immediately he began to search for evidence to establish exactly what took place in the alley. Anything would do right now, a torn fabric from the suspect's clothing, a weapon of some sort — something had to have been left behind

Two squad cars, an ambulance, and an unmarked sedan pulled up on the crime scene. Immediately a team of police officers and detectives went to work. They questioned anyone who stood around including people who lived in or worked around the area. The paramedics immediately confirmed that the woman had been dead for a couple of hours. Hearing this, Graham looked at his partner, hoping that the kid was paying attention to what was being said.

Intuition told him that the guy in the alley was probably innocent. Aside from the obvious details of the crime scene, the man in the alley was still a prime suspect. If he were truly innocent, he shouldn't have just fled the scene. Graham was able to get a good look of the guy. After giving the detectives an accurate description of the suspect and his last direction of travel, he and Baker were allowed to leave the scene.

John was certain that the combined efforts of the police departments within the district would be sufficient in finding the perpetrator of the crime. He replayed the events which had occurred in his mind, but none of it seemed to add up. John had almost allowed his doubt to override everything that he had seen that night until he began have the feeling as though he was being watched. Instinctively, he looked up into the rain-filled sky and saw a man peering down at him from the rooftops. A flash of lightning briefly illuminated the sky around a dark figure that stood carelessly on the ledge of an abandoned warehouse six stories above the crime scene. John brushed the rain from his eyes and narrowed his vision. Even in the storm, he was able to see the man's long silvery hair and dazzling eyes which held his gaze.

There was an additional flash of lightning, and the man on the rooftop disappeared. A bewildered Officer Graham paused in disbelief then returned to his squad car. He pulled out a pen and jotted down a few notes in the notebook he carried. Baker sat in the passenger seat rubbing an ice pack on the back of his head. John could see that he was itching to say something.

Before Baker could utter a word he held up one hand and shook his head saying. "Don't ask, Kid, just don't ask!" I can't explain what went on here tonight any better than you can. I have a feeling we are going to see our mystery man again sooner or later. That much you can count on, and don't worry... I won't tell the guys about how you got your ass kicked back there. Oh yeah, by the way you passed your final examination— welcome to the team. Baker shrugged his shoulders and turned his gaze back towards the alley. John placed the car's transmission into gear and slowly drove off. With all of the paper work he would have to do, this was definitely going to be a longer night than he expected

CHAPTER 3
Eyes of the Beholder

I walk the streets among you like a man bound to the earth. With each step that I take, my supernatural senses are bombarded by the sounds and smells of this city and its human inhabitants. Each mortal that crosses my path yields his thoughts to me willingly as I scan his mind for images of the elusive ones I track. This is a very simple trick that I have learned employ at will. Although it's more passive than any other ability I possess, I value it all the same because it has aided me throughout the ages.

Humans never seem to know the damned when they see them. They are usually so preoccupied with their own issues that they don't care about anything else that goes on around them. Through a human's eyes, I have the power to see my enemies. Even if they come into contact with humans for an instant, I can feel their dark presence and follow it to the source. In short, when it serves my purpose your thoughts, memories and all of the secrets you hide from the world become my own. I assure you, it happens swiftly and painlessly. It's almost like opening the pages of a book. I can absorb this information faster than you can possibly imagine.

I have witnessed humanity's birth into the world, and now more than ever I find myself in awe of your tenacity for survival and ingenuity. I have beheld with my angelic eyes many of the wonders that men have brought forth over the ages. Though I have watched and marveled at the vastness of God's grace, I dare not say that I have the complete understanding of His plan in regards to mankind. I can feel waves of His divine power emanating from them. In some it is stronger than others. Yet all beings created by Him possess an aura that surrounds and binds them all together.

It is like an intricate web of life that has endured since the first line of man, a living light that I can see and feel. Even the hell spawn possesses a similar essence, but of a darker nature. That is how I've hunted them for so long over the corners of the earth.

Now I am drawn closer to an even greater source of evil, one that has eluded me for centuries until now. Now it no longer seeks to lurk in the shadows. This is an evil which brings its touch of death into the light of day. With each life that it takes I'm drawn closer to it. This demon I pursue is more powerful than others I have faced before. I can feel its menacing presence, and I know its thoughts because his mind is open, unafraid, taunting me--even daring me to face him. I sense his overwhelming desires. The two most repetitive thoughts which flood his twisted mind are his "need to be worshiped by all and, most importantly, to be feared!"

All Walks Of Life

A tall, silver-haired figure stands in front of the window of an electronics department store, located on the corner of 4th and Main Street, right in the heart of the downtown Jersey City business district. Raziel stands in amazement, fixated by the various state-of-the-art electronic gadgets on display. The entire window is filled with television sets of all shapes and sizes, all of which are broadcasting the latest news, popular talk shows, and evening dramas.

To his right is a talk show in progress. The topic of discussion is centered on teenage girls who prefer dating older men. The overall scene is a complete moral disaster.

On stage are girls, no more than sixteen years old, parading around in front of a live television audience dressed in skimpy clothing. When brought out from their waiting rooms backstage, each one came out prepared to defend themselves. They yelled back obscenities to disapproving men and women who were in attendance. More than once a feminine body part was displayed in an act of vulgar defiance. If that spectacle weren't enough, the hostess of the show brought out the parents who were ashamed of their daughters' behavior. On opposing panels, sat close friends who altogether condoned, even encouraged the actions of the minors. The show was bound to result in chaotic scenes of violence erupting on the set.

More than once during the course of the show, the security team was called into action. Big burly men leaped into action to separate catfights and verbal altercations between a guest on the panel or some raving lunatic from the audience. To his left Raziel witnessed another talk show in progress called "Come Clean." The topic was based around transsexuals who were in serious relationships with partners that were unaware of their true sexuality. This particular talk show host was extremely crafty and a master at making difficult situations more complicated. He was the type of guy who did everything in his power to perpetuate obscene behavior simply for the purpose of receiving higher viewer ratings, the more scandalous the topic of discussion, the better the show.

The host had already set the tone for the show with the colorful introduction of his guest. Within seconds of his introduction, a gorgeous woman was escorted to her seat causing mixed reactions from the audience. Deborah Stevens was the post-operation transsexual who wanted to make a public confession to her husband regarding her true sexual nature. The audience made cruel remarks as the guest speaker painfully tried to explain the complexities of a being in a relationship based on lies. The host managed to settle the unruly crowd down, and the woman was able to proceed free of interruption.

As she spoke of her spouse, the cameraman switched to a hidden camera that had been focused on a simple looking man who sat in a secluded portion of the studio. He was dressed in a flannel shirt and trousers, wearing thick bifocal glasses. It was obvious that he was totally unaware as to why he was present and what was about to take place. The man just sat there in the back room waiting to be reunited with his loved one.

Raziel continued to watch the television program intensely, taking in depth the full measure of the man dressed in drag. Numerous medical operations consisting of breast implants and cosmetic reconstructions of the cheekbone and jaw line had created what sat before the television audience as a perfected picture of feminine beauty.

Deborah Stevens was the name of the exceptionally tall and curvaceous transsexual who sat bearing her heart before the audience. Her long blonde hair and enticingly deceptive blue eyes accentuated her other feminine features. Deborah began to tell the story of how she and her unsuspecting husband Frank first met. Three years ago she was a dancer working at an exotic nightclub called the Pink Flamingo in Las Vegas.

It was there that she met a clean-cut business executive who was in town for a two day convention. She was a little reluctant at first in giving any major details of her past, but slowly she began to describe how different he was compared to all the men who frequently patronized the nightclub. That same night after her performance was over, he met her at the foot of the stage and offered to buy her a drink. She accepted, and after a couple of rounds Frank had successfully broken through her defensive wall. Deborah elaborated further to the audience, saying with a smile how Frank initially came off like a geek.

However, the two of them shared one stimulating conversation after another until the bar closed.

"It had been a long time since anyone treated me that way," Deborah said. Most of the time it was the same old "let's go back to my room for sex" conversation that she was accustomed to hearing. Thinking back on it, Deborah really couldn't blame any of the men who came to the Pink Flamingo for acting that way. She remembered countless nights sitting at a table, wearing nothing more than a topless bikini, with large plumed peacock feathers attached to her headdress. "That's normally what all the Las Vegas showgirls would wear," she said, looking over to her host who sat crossed-legged, bent on her every word.

"The only things that covered my breasts were these huge star-shaped glitter stickers. Each one was placed directly over a nipple, but all that didn't seem to matter to Frankie! He was so different, the guy actually made me feel normal. He made me feel like a woman and not a freak with big tits!"

Deborah recalled how Frank had returned the following night just to tell her that he was leaving the next morning for Rhode Island. Frank had put all his cards on the table before they parted company, telling her that he wanted them to remain in contact with one another. He went on and on about how he enjoyed their previous conversation together and how it would be a shame for it to end so abruptly.

For some time Deborah had spoken the audience, and it seemed as if they forgot about the deception that had brought her to the show. As she poured her heart out, they seemed to listen sympathetically. It seemed as though her story was having a warming effect over them. Deborah became more emotional with each passing moment; she started weeping and seemed more apprehensive about coming forth with her confessions. The talk show host urged her to continue on with her story. Only after retrieving a napkin from her purse and wiping away her tears, did she continue.

Deborah knew that Frank actually thought she was a woman. She also knew that with each passing moment their mutual attraction grew. Deep down inside, Deborah knew the whole affair was leading to something that would be harder to explain in the end. Even though on the outside she could pass for a woman, Deborah was a man in possession of a penis. Previously, Deborah had several cosmetic surgeries, adding full and voluptuous breasts to a now shapely feminine body. In addition to the breast implants, Deborah had undergone cosmetic and reconstructive facial surgery, removing any unsightly facial hair and smoothing out his jaw line. Ultimately, it gave him a more sensual and womanly appearance.

Their last evening together ended with their having a romantic candle-light dinner at his suite in the Marriott. After several bottles of champagne, they began to engage in personal intimacies. Deborah used all of her skill in concealing her true nature. Driven by his insatiable desire to have sex, Frank pressed and probed fiercely at Deborah's body.

He kissed and touched her in places where she would allow. For an hour he attempted to grope at her inner thighs, seeking to penetrate with trembling fingers the place where her vagina should be. Each time his hands wandered down to her thighs, she pulled them away. After his failed attempts at initiating intercourse, Frank sat up, turned on the lights, and looked at her, "Why are you doing this?" Frank said. "Why tease me like this? If you don't want this to happen, then I will stop, but please don't continue to torture me like this."

Frank stood up and walked away from the bed and stood next to the floor-length glass window. Beyond the window lay the city of Las Vegas decked out in all its colorful splendor. At this vantage point on the twenty-eighth floor, the world below seemed to be a myriad of flashing lights, filled with people who scurried about like insects.

Deborah eyed Frank carefully through his reflection in the mirror. His face looked like a grim contemplating mask, one which spoke silently to her words he didn't have the heart to say. She knew that he had become frustrated and impatient with her, probably even questioning his own actions in bringing her to his suite.

Deborah stood up and walked over to him placing her hands around his waist.

Slowly she began to caress his chest biting the back of his neck ever so lightly. She continued to move her hands down towards his pants unfastening the device on his belt buckle. Placing her hands down his pants, she wasn't surprised to find an erect and throbbing penis lying in wait.

"You don't have to do this," Frank said as he allowed her to lead him back to the king-size bed.

"I do what I want, when I want!" Deborah replied as she pushed him backwards onto the mattress. "What followed next I will leave to your imagination," Deborah said as she looked at the audience who sat listening with their mouths gaped wide open. At this point in her story, it was clear that she held a captive audience. Many of them were fascinated; more than anything, they were disappointed by her reluctance to continue.

"Ok, I'll tell you the rest," she said. "When I finally decided to give in, I gave Frank an intense hour of oral sex. I was able to bring him to the point of climax and beyond. After it was all over, Frank was definitely satisfied. Nevertheless, he proceeded to ask me the inevitable question of why we didn't go all the way."

Deborah gave momentary pause to this inquiry. "The only answer I could give him was that I didn't want to rush into things. I lied my ass off when I told him that I wanted to have a commitment before giving myself to a man. Being the nice guy that he is, surprisingly, Frank bought into my story. I guess he didn't want to ruin the moment, so he left it alone. It didn't make me feel even better though. I can't imagine telling Frank the whole truth about what I am. I told myself over and over that it didn't matter because he was leaving and I would never see him again. In a couple of months, I would have the money that I needed to complete the sex change operation."

While the story was being unveiled to millions of viewers around the country, Frank sat patiently in the waiting room. His friends had warned him against going through with attending the show. It was a known fact that the show had a bad track record when it came to solving domestic issues.

Nevertheless, Frank wanted to be there for Deborah with his total support, intent upon the fact that no confession she made today would make him turn his back on their relationship. Deborah summed up her tale by saying how for the next five months they resumed with a sex-free long distance relationship, a relationship which led up to a long-anticipated sex change operation.

After three months of post-operation convalescence, she was reunited with Frank who returned to Las Vegas with a marriage proposal, one which Deborah hesitantly accepted. After it was all said and done, Deborah found herself telling one lie after the next to cover up her secrets. She lied about her family, saying that she had never known her biological parents. She claimed to have been raised in foster homes until she was seventeen years old. On a mid summer's day she left behind all she had ever known of the small town in Missouri and hitched-hiked west, landing one odd job after the next until she made it to Las Vegas.

Deborah broke down to the audience, proclaiming how she was being mentally and emotionally overwhelmed by her deception, and she knew there was only one way to end the circle of lies and put away her pain.

Up until now, she lived day-to-day with unbearable guilt. It would be through this talk show that she would attempt to make a long and overdue confession to the man she loved. The time had come for the blue-collar computer programmer from New Providence, Rhode Island to be summoned to the panel.

A man whom the talk show host introduced as Frank Thompson enthusiastically came out from behind a concealed partition. He walked proudly out to the set smiling and waving to an audience that greeted him with boisterous applause and whistles.

Deborah stood up eager to greet her husband with passionate kisses and embraces to the unsuspecting eye, it would appear that this show was actually doing a good deed by reuniting a happy couple. Yet underneath the lights and warm receptions, this was nothing more than a breeding ground for controversy and deception. After a lengthy commercial break, the show continued.

Words didn't come easy for Deborah who staggered around the subject of why she brought her husband to the show. Despite the courage she previously had shown, she seemed to lack the nerve to tell the truth altogether. After an evasive flow of confessions of how much she loved him, Deborah finally admitted to being a man, giving Frank all of the details of her deception.

Immediately, Frank stood up out of his chair in utter shock of what was said to him. The talk show host made an attempt at adding drama to the moment. Slowly, he walked towards Frank with both arms held out in an attempt to restrain him if necessary. Frank could do nothing more than look at his estranged wife in utter disbelief.

As for Deborah, she was devastated by his rejection and began to weep uncontrollably. The resolve she once possessed had definitely been shattered by his reaction. The talk show host began to whisper soothingly into the microphone telling Frank that he should remain calm. He wanted Frank to look over at the woman whom he had only moments ago had confessed his love to. Almost as if on cue to what was said, Deborah let out a loud, ear-piercing wail and fell out of her chair onto the floor. This had to be the worst display of acting that anyone had ever seen.

Raziel turned around to see a small crowd which had gathered around the store window, watching the program intensely, captivated by the entire spectacle that unraveled before them. An elderly man that stood next to him looked up and smiled, saying, "You gotta be careful with the women you chose today, son. You can't tell what you get until it's too late.

That one there could have fooled tha hell out of me too. Between you and me, I'd do her anyway (snicker)."

Raziel just gave a blank and uninterested glance at the man then turned his attention back to the fiasco unraveling on the screen. The whole set was in an uproar, Frank, who was standing in utter shock and disbelief seconds before, was now in a berserk rage. He was throwing chairs at the talk show host who now cowered in fear behind his stage security. The entire audience were on their feet screaming and yelling in approval of the chaos on stage.

People both young and old, were jumping up and down in a total frenzy. Frank had managed to break through security and grab the talk show host by the throat. The television audience went hysterical at this, and so did the small crowd behind Raziel.

Deborah had jumped on the back of her husband trying to restrain him as he continued with his assault on the terrified talk show host. The crowd went absolutely wild and now everyone was on their feet. The scene reminded Raziel of the crazed mobs and gladiatorial spectacles held at the Roman Coliseum in ancient times. Even the crowd that gathered behind him was ecstatic; they echoed the same exact chants that the frenzied talk show audience did.

Abruptly, the scene on the television changed from that of the talk show to one of a female news journalist reporting a live special news bulletin:

"This is Maria Calderon from channel six Action News. This is a special police Bulletin. Today marks the third week of random serial killings that have been plaguing the metropolitan area. This week alone the killer has claimed the lives of three women whose identities have yet to be released to the public. For fear of compromising ongoing investigations, police officials from the 32nd Precinct and the FBI are hesitant to release to the public detailed information concerning these acts of violence,. Nevertheless, police officials have left us with an image and description of a man they think may be the perpetrator of the crime."

The television screen flashed to reveal a drawing, which had been made by a police sketch artist displaying a crude image which resembled Raziel. Beneath the picture listed the physical descriptions stated by the police officer that gave a first person account.

Height:	6ft. 5in.
Weight:	225 lbs.
Age:	19-25
Eye Color:	Grayish Blue
Hair Color:	Silver

If you have any information regarding the whereabouts of this man, please call the Metropolitan Police Department citizens crime watchers hotline at 555-2677. Once again, the police authorities would like you to exercise extreme caution in dealing with this individual. He is considered armed and dangerous.

Because the image on the screen resembled him, Raziel looked at the screen in disbelief. He thought back to his encounter with the two mortals in the alley the previous night and knew it was they who accused him of this crime. Raziel turned around to see the crowd standing behind him as before. This time, however, he noticed that the expressions on their faces were not carefree as before. Now a more accusing and distrusting looks filled their faces.

Raziel scanned the minds of everyone who surrounded him, reading each of their thoughts one by one. He wasn't amazed to see how quickly humans drew their own conclusions in terms of innocence and guilt. Some even speculated the possibilities of gaining a reward from his capture. With little known facts, mankind was always quick to cast judgment. Despite his current situation, this was a matter well within his power to control. With very little effort, Raziel erased his image from their minds then instructed them to go on about their business.

After dispersing the crowd, Raziel surveyed the area one final time, ensuring that his presence went unnoticed. Then without warning, an electric shock went down his spine. Although uncomfortable, this experience was nothing new to him. He had felt this sensation countless times before. Closing his eyes, Raziel reached out with all of his angelic senses and knew that a source of great evil was drawing near.

The closer in proximity he came to it, the more frequent and potent his body spasms were. Raziel knew that this being of pure evil felt his presence as well. It had been this way since the very beginning. This was the uncommon physical reaction between the forces of light and creatures that dwell in shadow. Raziel lifted his arms and willed himself into the air then disappeared into the clouds. Bound by his eternal oath Raziel soared high above the city like a bird of prey seeking out the demon whose venomous touch flowed through the city bringing death to all it encountered.

CHAPTER 4
Sacred Order of The Illuminate

11:30 a.m. Eastern European Time
Vatican City Rome: Mother House of the Illuminate

A steady succession of footsteps moved leisurely across polished marble floors. Completely isolated from the modern day hustle and bustle of Rome, it is here that a remote compound called the Mother House of the Illuminate is located. For over a thousand years it has stood erect and defiant, its boundaries extending out towards the Italian peninsula. Within its secure confines, both men and women alike go on about their day-to-day business. Each individual seems to possess a silent connection with everyone around him or her, appearing to be a part of a collective awareness.

Slightly, they lower their heads as they pass one another, a gesture of friendship and of trust. The sounds of lectures and debates can be heard in almost every direction. It is common to see people from all walks of life gathered here, all of them from different races and cultural backgrounds, yet sharing the same purpose, sharing information and the expansion of knowledge. This is the very essence of the Palatine University for higher learning, known exclusively by its members as the Mother House for the sacred Order of the Illuminate.

For over two and a half thousand years the Illuminate has existed and thrived on the concept of attaining knowledge and understanding. Its origins were established during a time when the Roman Empire began its gradual decline from power. Not soon after the death of Christ some Romans slowly began to adopt Christianity as their own religion.

Moreover, it was the doing of the Emperor Constantine who exhibited a lust for knowledge and curiosity, primarily in the death and resurrection of the Christian god. Constantine had endorsed intellectual missionaries to seek the answers to this enigma. Thus, the initial numbers of the Order was formed, spreading out across the ancient boundaries of the Roman Empire searching for knowledge of unexplained phenomena. Over the centuries, the Illuminate became more organized and their exploits were well financed by Constantine and the successors of his throne.

They were the most secret of organizations, accountable to no one save the select few royal magistrates who held a seat within the inner council of the imperial court.

Three hundred years after its formation, the Order of Illuminate was eventually placed under the direct responsibility of an individual who held a rank in Roman society second only to that of the Emperor. The eminent title of Pope was created to oversee the transition of the new Roman society from one that practiced the worship of false gods and idolatry to Christianity. High seated officials in the Illuminate in turn reported their findings directly to the Pope and he to the Emperor, who at this time had no real governing powers, yet served as a figurehead in Roman society.

Although the Illuminate was established during a time when the empire was slowly deteriorating, their selective membership was steadily increasing. The common liberal arts and sciences of the ancient world were theirs to examine and master. However, it was the activities of the unnatural world that held a particularly greater fascination to its members. For reasons long established by the fore bearers of the order, it was decreed that all who gained acceptance within the order would be chosen. No position of nobility or wealth could buy admittance within this secret society.

Those who were admitted within their fold were held to the most sacred of trusts. Their members took a vow of secrecy to never reveal their true nature to anyone outside of the sect, nor give any outsider insight to the secretive world of the Illuminate. Despite having to abide by countless rules where even curfews were strictly enforced, this world concealed within walls of stone and ancient secrecy held every necessity that life could offer.

This was especially true for Victor Bradley, a twenty-one year-old apprentice of the Illuminate. His is a path that had only begun within the order. Soon he would be made to face the embodiment of two extremes, ultimate good and evil. This is his story.

CHAPTER 4

Sacred Order of The Illuminate

Part II. Revelations

A rapid succession of footsteps raced across polished marble floors as Victor Bradley sprinted across the garden square of the Illuminate Mother house. He could feel his heart pounding fiercely while he held on to an international newspaper pressed tightly to his chest. Within seconds he entered the palazzo and continued his pace down the main hall. Tirelessly, he sprinted up two flights of stairs and continued to head towards the east wing of the estate. Until he reached the archives, Victor ran until he was nearly out of breath. It was a place of solitude, research, even meditation, where some of the most ancient texts and knowledge of the world were kept.

As Victor ran down the main hall of Palatine University, his thoughts were overflowing with unanswered questions and random images of recent murders bearing occult ritualistic similarities. "There are so many questions that need to be brought into clarity," Victor mumbled to himself. "Those mysteries, only Edward may bring into light." There was another matter that needed to be addressed, one that held an even greater concern for Victor.

Lately, the nightmares and visions he'd been able to

suppress for years had returned to haunt him again. Each night they grew stronger and more malign, even seemingly life-threatening. One nightmare continued to haunt his dreams. It was of the same dark specters that pursued him through a wilderness of scorched earth and chard decaying bodies. In this vision, Victor was barefoot, running through a burning forest. His eyes were irritated from the ash and smoke that surrounded him. Poisonous gasses filled his lungs, threatening to suffocate the life out of him.

Razor sharp thorns ripped at his flesh as he ran through a wall of thickets, attempting to escape death. Wicked voices screamed out hideous curses behind him, yet he ran, on ignoring the pain. Blood flowed down violently in pools from the cuts on his brow, falling into his eyes temporarily blinding him.

Faster and more desperately he ran, not knowing the direction in which he traveled. Deeper and deeper into the wall of thorns he pressed, until he could no longer move. All around him the voices and screams grew louder as the source of danger seemed to draw closer towards him. A net of thorns encircled him. Like a fly caught in the web of a spider, his arms and legs were trapped.

Imprisoned within this net of thorns, Victor saw before him a stone altar surrounded by dark and towering hooded men. Each of these figures was adorned in the attire similar to that of ancient pagan priests. Hanging from their necks were ceremonial jewels of their sect. Their pitch-black robes were lined with red velvet material of the finest quality; precious emeralds and blood sapphires ran down the length of these garments.

As one of the priests chanted a series of ceremonial rites in an ancient Latin dialect, Victor caught a glimpse of a sacrifice which lay bound upon their altar. Flames danced upon torches, which illuminated the unholy sacrificial circle. Victor was compelled to look on as though he was being mesmerized. With weary eyes he watched as thin wisps of smoke rose and drifted off into the darkness, the smoke and fire seemed to flicker in unison with the chants of the hooded priests. In the background Victor could hear drums beating violently. A steady rhythm flowed on repetitively as if its purpose was to aid in the evocation of an unknown force into the circle.

As the beating drums began to fade, the circular wall formed by the priests around the altar opened to reveal a little girl bound helplessly upon its surface. Victor's heart pounded harder than before. In this dream state, the little girl seemed familiar to him. His mind raced furiously trying to distinguish what significance she held to him. From her physical appearance, it was obvious that she could have been closely related to him. Victor's heart began to race as he felt sorrow for the girl. Her hands and feet were bound with the same cruel thorns that held him captive.

The child had a look of innocence blended with fear upon her face. She couldn't have been more than seven years old, Victor thought as he watched on with intent eyes. Her curly black hair was matted with leaves and dried blood. It appeared to Victor that she was captured in the wilderness and had been beaten within an inch of her life. Now it appeared as though she would serve as the sacrifice for the robed priests' evil designs.

For a brief moment, their eyes met. Victor could see that a single tear had formed in the wells of her eyes and had begun to roll down her dirty, scarred cheeks. Her body and spirit were weakened from the whole ordeal of her capture and abuse.

Yet despite her ill fate, she mustered enough strength to utter the words *"Help Me!"* from dry, cracked lips. This made Victor struggle even more to free himself of his bonds.

All of the efforts he made were in vain. The more he struggled, the tighter the bonds became. As if alive, a single cord of thorns wrapped itself around his neck, forcing his head to remain still and witness the sacrifice. Once more the eyes of the two captives met. All the while the drums and the chanting gradually died away.

The hooded figure that led the ritual walked towards Victor, revealing a long razor sharp dagger. With a tone filled with hatred and anger he began uttering a mass of jumbled words at him. In two rapid movements, he sliced both of Victor's wrists. Victor screamed out in pain as the blood gushed out from the gaping wounds. Immediately, the priest retrieved a large bowl to catch the river of blood. Raising his arms above his head, the robed figure began to chant more sacred rites. As he chanted, the cuts on Victor's wrist began to burn as if fire flowed across the wounds.

To Victor's surprise, however, the gashes began to seal themselves completely. It was as if his flesh was restored by black magic or some unholy sorcery used by the priest. Since the priest had turned and walked away, it seemed that his blood was all they required for the moment. He did not know if his life was to be forfeit as well to complete this ceremony.

Turning his attention to the circle of hooded figures, the High Priest walked towards the altar and drank a long drought of Victor's blood; then he passed it around to the others until its contents were consumed entirely.

The High Priest looked down at the stone slab upon which the small girl lay struggling. Slowly, he walked until he was standing directly over her. As he looked at his sacrificial lamb, he bent over and began to whisper softly in her ear. So low and secretive were his words that only the two of them could have possibly heard what was being said. After speaking to the child, the priest took his dagger and cut loose the bonds that held her captive.

Then he carefully lifted the child up from the altar and placed her on the floor. As gentle and caring as a father would have done, the priest stood behind the girl holding her by the shoulders. Bending over, the priest began whispering to her once more. Slowly, she began to nod her head up and down in acknowledgement. After placing the dagger within her small hands, the High Priest proceeded to lead her towards Victor.

"No!" Victor shouted. "Nora, you must fight this dark magic. Please don't do this. It is not our way! Our people are forbidden to go against the laws of Moses. It is forbidden! You must try to fight against it."

Surprised at his own words, Victor began to struggle, trying to free himself of his bonds and even of this dream. "This is only a dream," Victor thought to himself, but somehow it seemed as real as anything he'd ever known.

Closer and closer, Nora drew towards him repeating the chants of the hooded priest. Their words combined and flowed together in a rapid crescendo. As she repeated the rites, the drums beat as fiercely as before. Victor's heart pounded as he begged and pleaded for the girl to stop. Once within striking distance, the little girl looked innocently up at him and smiled. Slowly, she stood up on her tiptoes and kissed him gently on both cheeks. Looking deeply into his dark brown eyes, she thrust the dagger hard into his chest. Excruciating pain flowed through Victor's body!

Despite how painful his experience was, it was the only means of escape from this horrible nightmare. Victor immediately awoke from his dream drenched in sweat. He took the palm of his right hand and wiped the perspiration away from his brow. Gradually his heart rate began to slow down back to normal. Victor sighed a deep breath of relief, knowing that he was free, and that it was only a vision that held him prisoner. This was nothing more than an unfamiliar event from an uncertain past which haunted his subconscious mind.

Before the memory of danger could pass from his awakening consciousness, Victor turned over and reached for a thick leather-bound notepad and a pencil. Swiftly, he began to jot down the particulars of his dream. He sought to accurately recount and document every detail of his vision. This was something Victor has done since he was a child. His mentor taught him how to focus on the visions and decipher their truer meanings, no matter how odd or obscure they seemed. Pausing momentarily, he looked out of the window and marveled at the silvery light of the full moon being cast inside his room. After completing his journal entry, he closed the notepad.

In the dim illumination he noticed a fresh scar that ran across the back of his hand. The wound itself was an inch in length, and a thin line of blood trickled down its surface. Stricken with panic, Victor rose from his bed and walked towards the bathroom located within his quarters. After turning on the light, he noticed more tiny scratches and bruises on his face and arms. He looked down at his feet and noticed that they were caked with mud.

"Impossible!" Victor said out loud to himself. As he looked at his reflection in the mirror, he tried to come up with a rational explanation for his present condition. He immediately came up with sleep walking as a reasonable theory. Victor turned on the faucet and began to talk to himself as he cleaned his wounds. "Get a hold to yourself, Victor. Not only do I have freaky visions from past lives to deal with, but I'm starting to walk in my sleep as well!"

Victor took a handful of cold water and began to douse his face, trying to regain his wits. He let the water flow through his palms for a few seconds, enjoying the sensation as it numbed his fingers. He closed his eyes and stared to breathe in deep breaths, trying to calm himself down and tap into rational thoughts. "Almost there," Victor said to himself as he slowly opened his eyes hoping to have regained all control of his emotions.

As he looked up at the mirror, his heart jumped in reaction to the image of a hooded figure lurking in the shadows behind him. It seemed to peer at him with fire red orbs filled with menace from across the distance. Quickly, Victor turned around, absolutely surprised to find nothing but an empty space where the man had once stood. Frantically, he searched every corner of his room for traces of an intruder; none could be found.

"Great, now I'm beginning to hallucinate!" Victor said. "I need to Focus and clear my mind!" In the light of the moon, Victor sat cross-legged in the middle of his room, taking in deep breaths, focusing his thoughts, and directing his psyche. Over the years within the Illuminate, he learned to tap into the recesses of his mind and unleash his telepathic abilities. From within, he opened his thoughts in waves and sent them outwards, scanning his surroundings. Then pushing his abilities to their limits, he reached out further towards the woods which lay out in the distance.

His thoughts pierced the shadows over one hundred yards away from his window. Victor was able to project his psychic thought waves out like radar; in return he sensed nothing more than the random movements of small animals scurrying for food. Occasionally he would catch remnants of unshielded thoughts from someone who was within the range of his telepathic scan. The thought of eavesdropping on one of his peers troubled him.

As a result of this momentary loss of concentration, his thoughts instantly receded back to their source. Satisfied that there was no danger within his immediate area, Victor stood up and walked to a cabinet filled with linen. After he picked out a fresh set, he returned to his bed to replace the soiled sheets.

Victor began to reflect back to a time when he was young, afraid, and had no one to help him control the visions that came from within. In the days of his youth, he had similar dreams where he would rise from his sheets screaming out at the top of his lungs. Victor could recall having visions and nightmares since he was three years old.

He reflected back to when he first arrived at the order. After hearing one of his outbursts, a school master on night patrol of the compound raced into his room. Seeing that it was only a child's dream that was the cause for alarm, the master scholar dismissed the incident, viewing it only as a sign of his not being able to adjust.

With the exception of Edward Wiltshire, no one would listen or help Victor seek clarity in his nightmares. Edward was a powerful psychic and elder of the Illuminate who chose to be Victor's mentor and guide within the order. Over the years Victor had learned to discern between what was real and the things that were false when he dreamt. His prophetic visions had always seemed realistic but as of late certain elements would always manifest themselves in his dreams. The little girl and the robed priest were always there and a sacrifice that required bloodshed would always take place.

Thinking back on it all, he connected these dreams with his acceptance into the order as an apprentice. As a child he lived in England with an uncle who worked late hours at a textile factory. His parents were killed in a car accident when he was very young. The eldest brother of his mother took legal guardianship of him up until he was eight years old. This was around the time when his revelations started getting worse.

His uncle wasn't a patient man and each night when Victor slept his dreams would come and he would wake screaming in terror. For months this occurred, and Victor's Uncle left him to the care of medical physicians and psychologists. After their combined analysis and theories had been exhausted, none of them could not come up with a logical explanation for the vivid accounts Victor gave of his nightmares. No one could see how one so young could imagine such horrible things and never deviate from the story. Victor's consistencies were mind-boggling.

An anonymous yet wealthy benefactor, hearing of the child's dreams, offered his uncle a small fortune to take the exceptional child into his care. The man proposed to take Victor to a private institution where he would receive treatment for the mental unrest he displayed. Along with medical treatment, the benefactor also guaranteed that all of Victor's other needs would be met at no cost to his family. After hearing the man's proposal, Victor's uncle jumped at the opportunity to free himself of his burden.

Victor remembered being led out of the hospital with his belongings stuffed in a burlap sack. There was a nurse and a doctor who accompanied him to the breezeway of the building where a limousine awaited to him. A tall elderly man in a tweed tailor made suit stood outside smoking a pipe greeted the medical officials with a smile. After they had exchanged words and the man had signed all of the necessary documents they were on their way. During the entire ride to the airport the old man glanced down at a gold pocket watch that was attached to his blazer.

Every now and then he would glance over at his new ward and smile warmly but there was no real lengthy exchange of words between the two them. Once Victor saw the private jet that they were about to board his curiosity and excitement peaked. Once aboard the vessel their journey to Rome was underway. Victor was inquisitive by nature and as a result he bombarded his escort with a barrage of questions. His primary concern was The names and ages of the children where they were going. Victor made it a point to inform the man who sat next to him how much he much liked eating ice cream, adding specific details of how his uncle never allowed him to eat ice cream before bedtime.

Periodically during the flight, an attendant would pass by his seat and find herself amazed at Victor's intelligent conversational skills. He became an instant favorite among the other crew members as well. Throughout the trip, at least a half dozen attractive flight attendants brought snacks and cooed over him., Victor rambled on and on about things which for an eight year old would seem to be of great importance. Unlike Victor's uncle, the elderly man who sat next to him proved to be a very patient and pleasant man. When asked questions, he would smile warmly and give answers to the best of his ability. He made a point of telling his young ward everything he needed to know until Victor was satisfied and fell asleep.

After a few hours of driving across the countryside, Victor gazed out of the window of the restored 1950-style Rolls-Royce. As the miles passed by, he watched in amazement at the cattle and other livestock that grazed along the green pastures. Once they arrived at their destination, Victor's eyes lit up at the size of the Palatine estate. He could almost imagine all of the great adventures he would have playing with the other children in the well-maintained gardens.

Holding Victor's hand, the old man stood at the threshold of the Illuminate's main entrance and formally introduced himself to his new ward. "Victor, my name is Sir Edward

Wiltshire the Third. You may call me Edward. I will be your guide within the order and in time hopefully you will consider me your friend. There is something special that you carry within you, a power that I would like to help you control. I know about the dreams that cause you not to sleep at night. Together we may be able to make those bad dreams go away. You would like that wouldn't you?"

Nodding his head slowly up and down, Victor gave his silent reply.

"Good!" Edward said. "Now with that over and done with, we can start things off properly. How would you like to go to the kitchen and see if we can find some ice cream?" Young Victor jumped up and down overjoyed, and after taking Edward's hand he was led within the confines of the estate for ice cream. Afterwards, he was taken to his quarters to drop off the personal items that he carried with him. From that moment on, Victor was quite the student. With ease he learned to speak fluent Hebrew and Latin. His curiosity over the years continued to grow with his need for knowledge. He soon forgot about his darker days with his uncle in England.

Under the tutelage of his Master and the order, Victor grew into manhood. With the exception of his dreams, all darkness seemed to have faded away. Those he eventually learned to control and document keeping a thorough log of each event. Within time his lessons became more advanced, and he marveled at the dormant mental abilities that Edward helped him to unlock. Now as he drifted off to sleep, Victor felt content with these thoughts of his past. There was also an even greater sense of security in knowing how far he'd come in such a short time.

It was during times like these when he sought answers to questions that eluded him. His visions were beginning to manifest themselves into pieces of a bigger puzzle. Each night a clue was revealed to him. He could hardly wait until the morning when he would go to Edward and tell him every detail of his vision, and even the specter that appeared to him the previous night.

There was a quote Edward frequently used to set his mind at ease at times like these: "Tomorrow is only a day away, and with the rising of a new sun comes a lesson that can be learned." On this very thought, Victor closed his eyes and knew peace as he slept though the night.

Chapter 5

The Quest

"Edward's meditation chamber is near!" Victor said to himself as he made his way down a long elaborate corridor of polished mahogany walls. In the countless times he had made this trip, Victor never really took a second look at the priceless items and oil paintings which were hung about nonchalantly in every direction. Everything here had been collected over the centuries and was part of the Illuminate's archives. From the vase displayed upon a pedestal in front of a window, to the 12th century tapestry which hung on the wall, everything here was significant and had been acquired during a specific time for a specific reason. Victor thought, "If these things were appraised, they would be worth millions."

Finally, Victor stood outside the door of a chamber where an elderly man pored over scrolls and texts written in ancient Sumerian. After waiting for a few moments to catch his breath and regain his composure, Victor quietly entered the room. He was about to extend a formal and respectful greeting, when the elder whose back was turned to him raised a single hand, beckoning for him to remain silent. Not seeming to break his concentration as the old man continued to examine the manuscript, looking back and forth, the man shifted uneasily in his chair as he pored over the frail documents. At each passing moment, Victor's curiosity began to build. He wanted to know exactly what it was that held his master's attention so firmly.

Victor looked over his master's left shoulder and saw an old chart of the constellations which had been made before the renaissance period. Next to the star chart were two additional scrolls that bore cuneiform and hieroglyphic symbols on them. Victor was unable to decipher the full meaning of the documents that were laid before him, but he noticed that two of the scrolls bore similarities in their overall theme. They were in fact representations of an ancient gathering of some sort.

The document which held his master's attention contained a depiction of the struggle between good and evil. There was a scene within this scroll where a man stood concealed behind a large bolder in the desert; he was witnessing a winged creature of great stature handing a dagger-like object to a priest. Before he could make out any more of the scrolls' details, the old man gathered them up carefully and covered them.

Then he turned his attention towards Victor and said, "Young man, why do you insist on disturbing me in such a fashion? When I was a young apprentice, one would never seek out a master in meditation; such a thing was unheard of!"

Victor only smiled at his master's words for he knew their only intent was to mildly scold him for his abrupt intrusion.

Sir Edward Wiltshire was a picture-perfect distinguished English gentleman. Well into in his late sixties, his hair was full yet gray; a pair of simple round spectacles sat firmly on the bridge of his nose. Despite his sharp wit and vast intellectual powers, his vision was not as sharp as it used to be. In fact, without his specs he was certifiably blind.

Nevertheless, Edward's strength in character and wisdom solidified his position within the order. Since he was twenty-three Edward had been a revered member of the order. In fact, everywhere he went his reputation preceded him. All that knew him had a great level of love and respect for him.

Eleven years had passed since the day that he had brought

Victor to the towering gates of the Illuminate. Despite his regular intrusions, Edward was thoroughly pleased with the young man who stood before him. Victor was the most gifted apprentice he'd ever taught.

By this point in their relationship, the two of them were well beyond the use of words. Edward knew that whenever his apprentice would seek him out in the midst of his study, it was usually because he had discovered something that needed to be explained. After looking his young apprentice over, he turned his attention to the newspaper article the young man clung to so desperately. Reaching out and grabbing it with a speed deceptive of his aged appearance, he began to examine the article.

He began to pore over every inch of the document. Within moments he looked over the brim of his glasses at Victor and gave a smile of approval. Victor knew that his master was pleased with his finings and had drawn an assumption similar to his own. In the years spent under the direct tutelage of his mentor, Victor knew things which apprentices new to the order were forbidden to know.

These were certain rules of the order, where gaining knowledge was like a rite of passage which came with years. The longer one was in the order, the more information he had access to. In this particular situation, this was a rule that Edward chose to overlook when it came to his relationship with Victor.

When he took Victor under his care, he revealed to him the lost texts of Hereticus. Hereticus was a pagan priest from ancient Greece and the founder of a cult long forgotten by historians called Heretics. It is said that he lived eight hundred years before the birth of Christ. Some believed that he was an oracle who could see the future and guide the lives of men; others thought that he was a raving lunatic who sought fortune by telling people what they wanted to hear. Hereticus claimed to have witnessed in a vision the birth of creation and the struggle between good and evil. So compelling were these visions that he became absorbed with them and began to relish thoughts of attaining godlike power.

It wasn't long before Hereticus had a gathering of followers who shared his beliefs. Over a thousand years his cult numbers multiplied. They easily deceived the power-hungry men of the world into doing their bidding.

Such pagan cults of worship were born where hundreds even thousands of mortals pledged their loyalty to fallen angels who seemed as gods to them. Desperately foolish men and women sold their souls to their new masters, forfeiting everlasting paradise for short-lived wealth and power.

Seen later by the secular world as the father of the occult, Hereticus was held in the highest regard. His life would be forever shrouded in mystery. On his deathbed a demon of immense power revealed himself to Hereticus offering to have his wildest dreams come true. Desperate for eternal life and power, he foolishly accepted the demon's dark gift, becoming a soulless slave for the creatures of shadow for all time.

During the period in history known as the dark ages, all knowledge of Hereticus had faded out of the memory of man. It would not be for another thousand years before any trace of his order would surface. Remnants of the Heretic order were eventually found on the black market. Its delicate scrolls were purchased by an anonymous private collector who spent a large portion of an inheritance originating from English nobility in collecting these documents. It was the scrolls of Hereticus that Edward read from regularly within the secluded chambers of the Illuminate.

He exercised every precaution being in being careful not to fall prey to the fantastical elements and beliefs of this cult. Edward took a particular interest in one text which spoke of adversaries to the dark lords, those who made attempts at preventing the coming of the new age where their rapidly diminishing numbers would be rendered to dust and few select men and women would evolve, becoming the new gods of the Earth.

Holding the article that he had taken from his apprentice, Edward Wiltshire stood in amazement. He could not help but to notice the distinct markings left upon the body of the slain woman in the picture. He had seen markings like those before. Edward's mind raced backwards in time, recounting his earlier years within the Illuminate. After decades of researching though hundreds of textbooks containing ancient hieroglyphics and cuneiform, he knew the markings inscribed on the woman were not of this world.

Edward fumbled through a leather-bound bag and pulled out a book which contained clippings from textbooks and newspaper articles he had collected over the years. One particular article had a picture of similar markings carved onto the body of a little Jewish boy in Germany. The article was written during the Adolph Hitler rise to power over sixty years ago.

Another article containing pictures of these symbols were found on a young woman who had been slain in Central Park during the early seventies. Police authorities apprehended a suspect who turned himself in for the crime and was later determined mentally insane. It was later found that the man claimed responsibility for the murder did so in the hopes of seeking notoriety for himself. All of this occurred during the investigations of the Son of Sam murders in New York City. According to the article in Edward's possession, the same grotesque murder has been recently committed several different times in areas within and surrounding Jersey City. Glancing down at the article, Edward began to speak with slow, measured words.

"For years I have studied the relics from ancient civilizations, pouring over scrolls and ancient tablets for the truth of what we are and how we came to be. Within these very walls are documents that survived the infamous flames that erupted in Queen Cleopatra's royal libraries. So many secrets have remained here within our order safely for over a thousand years. Everything you see here has been procured hundreds of years ago and passed down from one scholar to the next bound by the most sacred of trusts."

As he spoke, his eyes grew wide with astonishment. "No theological or scientific theory has brought me closer to having those questions answered than what you see before you," Edward said as he looked up at Victor and back down at the pile of scrolls. "From the time I received my initial lessons here within these walls, the elder scholars always insisted the path to true knowledge lay in the East. How wrong they were. Victor, we shall rewrite that old theory!"

Standing up, he gathered all the documents which were spread across the table and placed them within a airtight metallic container. Then he placed the container and its fragile contents in a vault.

"Preparations must be made and precautionary measures must be taken to prevent this information falling into the wrong hands. The answers we seek are currently in the West and there is where we must go." Edward seemed extremely excited and a bit nervous as he moved around the chamber gathering his personal belongings. He headed towards the door to leave but stopped dead in his tracks and turned to face Victor, saying,

"You must not say a thing to anyone concerning what was revealed to you within this chamber today. Is that clear? This matter is extremely delicate for anyone to know of except the inner council."

Edward paused for a moment then softened his tone; he walked over to Victor and placed a hand on his shoulder. Looking his apprentice squarely in the eyes, he said, "Leave now and keep your peace. Do not speak of this to anyone and guard your thoughts as well. I will send for you after I attend to some affairs, all of which may take a couple of days at best. If you have kept this secret, by the time I return I will even include you into my plans."

Victor immediately swelled with excitement. "I swear to you, Edward; no one will know of this. You have my word, and when you return I will be ready."

"Guard your thoughts carefully, young apprentice. Do not think randomly of this, and look for my return within the next forty-eight hours," Edward said as he walked past his apprentice, tossing the neatly folded newspaper over his left shoulder.

Caught off guard by the gesture, Victor looked down and mused over the newspaper which had the picture of a metropolitan city on the cover. By the time he looked up again Edward had disappeared among the crowded halls of the palazzo.

Immediately Victor created a mental barrier, forcing his mind to be closed to anyone who might seek to intrude upon his thoughts. Tucking the newspaper securely within his jacket, he strolled out towards the garden square. Soon his master would send for him, and he had every intention on being ready for any and everything that would follow.

CHAPTER 6

Servant of the Mark

10:30 a.m. Lower East side Jersey City
The sports stadium of New Providence Middle School was filled with teenagers who were engaged in an intense game of soccer. Unknown to everyone within the grounds, an ancient evil lay in wait. Concealed behind thick branches, twisted thoughts flowed through a tormented mind. Driven by his unquenchable blood lust, a powerful immortal named Mathias looks on with piercing eyes. For days he has stalked his prey, now he watches her patiently…waiting for an opportunity to strike

"I can't believe Veronica chose Sarah to be on her team instead of me!" said a young girl who stood alone, alienated and deep in thought. For half an hour she'd been trying very desperately to hold back her tears of frustration as she looked out at a group of her peers playing soccer. All the while, she brooded over her lack of popularity among her new classmates. Prior to arriving at her new middle school, Jessica Graham, like any other teenage girl, had numerous fantasies of fitting in.

Throughout the entire summer months, all Jessica could think about were the things she would be able to do and the new friends she would make. "Now things were going to be different," she thought to herself. Jessica was twelve years old now, a sixth grader, practically all grown up.

She began to reflect back to her past, a past filled with the painful memories of an irreplaceable loss and to a time when her father Jonathan Graham was a rookie cop new to the police force. Undoubtedly a strong bond was shared between the two. They were in fact all each other had. When she was three, Jessica's mother had been killed in the most violent way. She was young when it happened, but Jessica could vividly recall every moment they spent together up to the time of her passing.

Even as a child, Jessica had an uncanny awareness of her surroundings, and she played close attention to her father. There was a time when his face was always smiling and full of laughter; now he hardly smiled at all. Until the day comes when you are faced with it, no one really understands how it feels to lose a loved one,.

After losing her mother, Jessica saw how her father became absorbed, even obsessed in his work. For years he was bent on finding the ones responsible for the death of his wife. Jessica remembered times when she would find her father looking off into the distance, his eyes having an empty and distant look in them. Only the light tug of her small hands would bring him back to the present. It seemed like during those years, only she could to make him smile. Jessica started to think back on her first days of school and how her father filled out the documents for admittance during registration.

Occasionally a teacher would come near just to coo over her. She couldn't count the number of times she heard her name and the word *adorable* used in the same sentence. When approached, Jessica would latch on tighter to her father's pants and bury her head against his leg. She distinctly remembered how much she cried as her father took her to school in their old beat up Chevy Nova. Jessica remembered how all the other kids ran up to him that first day fascinated by his uniform.

Jessica could still smell the perfume of the tall and pleasant young woman who took her by the hand and with reassuring words led her into a colorful classroom. After being introduced to the class, the other children accepted her immediately.

Jessica began to smile even wider when she reflected back on one little boy in particular named Ryan who took an interest in her. He was extremely inquisitive and was bold enough to walk up and introduce himself. Immediately he began to ask her questions about where she lived and about her parents. Although Ryan appeared to be rather odd to her, the two played with one another throughout the course of the day.

She remembered correcting him several times in the correct way to say her name. After realizing he had a speech impediment, she settled with him calling her Jessie. Because of her new found best friend, that name that stuck with her throughout childhood. Jessie and Ryan became the best of friends. In fact, they were inseparable. They did almost everything together, Jessica laughed as she remembered how she would coax him into having tea parties, and he even convinced her to play on his little league soccer team.

"Those were good memories and better times," Jessie thought as she looked back over to the soccer field. "Moving to this new neighborhood isn't all that my dad said it would be.

I know that I'm better than half of the girls out there, but no one wants me on their team." Standing up, she grabbed a spare ball and began to kick it around. With deceptive skill, she maneuvered up and down the field kicking the soccer ball between her legs. Using her imagination, she envisioned an opponent directly in front of her guarding the imaginary goal that lay ahead. She scrambled to the left, dribbling the ball, then stopped and changed directions. She suddenly sped up and performed a trick by spinning around and kicking the ball with her left heel.

All the while, she kept the ball moving towards the goal. Biting down slightly on her lower lip, Jessica concentrated totally on scoring the winning point. Her imaginary defender advanced in on her swiftly with a slide tackle meant to take away the ball. In anticipation of the move, she locked down on the ball with both ankles and hopped upward in a half circular motion, landing gracefully on the ground, tapping the ball lightly with her right foot. Then she took another half step and drew back with all her might and kicked the ball with her left foot, sending it soaring into the imaginary net and deep into to woods that surrounded the playground.

"Smooth move, Ex-Lax," was the sarcastic comment that came from a group of girls who stood along the side lines watching as Jessica performed her complex acrobatic soccer moves. "Too bad you'll never get the chance to do those moves in a real game." More laughter erupted in the background as a lanky blonde haired girl with braces stepped forward and made her snide remarks directed at Jessica.

A whistle blew loudly from across the distance summoning everyone in from recess. A tall and very attractive black woman stood at the threshold of the school building. Long silky black hair, full lips, and hazel brown eyes accentuated her natural beauty. The woman was casually dressed wearing a pair of conservative slacks and a wool turtleneck sweater. Ashley Price was the name of the twenty-six year old substitute teacher who was definitely a favorite among all of the students, especially the males with their locker room talk and raging hormones. She was of black and Hispanic descent and was drop-dead gorgeous. Jessica's attention was drawn back to the present by more of the girl's snide comments.

Sara was now walking towards the building looking back talking over her shoulder, "Better hurry. You wouldn't want to be late for class, Super Star." Red faced with embarrassment, Jessica bit down on her lip again. "Why do I let her get to me like that?" Jessica thought to herself. The wind had begun to blow a little harder, and as Jessica looked up she could see the rain clouds starting to gather.

"Perfect; it's about to rain again!" Jessie said as she wiped the blonde hair away from her face. Now where did that ball go? She picked up her pace a light jog and ran in the direction where she saw it roll. The air around her was warm and was filled with the smell of rain that threatened to fall at any moment. The trees swayed back and forth with the breeze and the sun was hidden behind large gray rain clouds. Birds scurried from branch to branch as if disturbed by an unseen presence.

"Jessie, hurry up and come inside or you'll be late for class!" Miss Price was calling out to her from across the distance.

"I'll be there in a second," Jessie replied. I just have to grab this soccer ball. Walking towards the foot of the bushes, Jessica hesitated momentarily as she heard a rustling from within. Pausing, she looked around the area from left to right. The hairs on her arms and the back of her neck begin to rise.

"Get a hold of yourself, Jess, there's nothing to fear here." Reassured by her own words, she pressed on. Once within the thick foliage, she began to survey the ground for the ball. Slowly, she strayed deeper into the woods. Jessie let out a sigh of relief when she saw the ball half concealed within a patch of weeds less than fifty feet away.

"Whew. There you are," Jessica said as she ran towards the ball. Once more she heard Miss Price calling out to her from across the distance.

Jessie turned around to face the direction of the school. Cupping her hands around her mouth, she yelled back, "I'll be there in a second!"

As she turned around again, Jessie was startled by a towering man who stood directly in front of her holding the ball in the palm of his hand. He extended his arm out to its full length and said to her in a low calm voice, "I believe this belongs to you." Jessica's heart began to pound. Instinctively, she leapt backwards, tripping over a branch that lay upon the canvas. Dark green eyes peered down at her as he slowly made his advance. Jessica looked up and took in every detail of the huge man that walked towards her.

He was tall and well built. The man wore an expensive three-piece suit with a long overcoat. From his outward appearance, he was dressed like a Wall Street executive. His face was narrow with a chiseled jaw line and high forehead and arched brows. His skin was pale and looked smooth. It seemed to reflect the light as if it were polished marble. For the most part, he was fairly handsome.

His long, shiny blond hair was pulled back in a ponytail with the exception of two long, thin bangs that he allowed to hang freely in his face. His eyes were intense and focused. Their color was like an emerald green gem that reflected the light. A hint of darkness and menace seemed to pour out from behind their sockets.

A smile appeared on his face as though he enjoyed seeing the fear of her reaction. White teeth flashed as he laughed openly at her. For a moment Jessica thought that she had caught a glimpse of tiny fangs peering at her from the corners of his mouth. With one hand he covered his mouth as he continued his erratic laughter. Jessie sat up on her hands and looked crossly up at him. She began to feel the blood rush to her face she turned red with anger.

Jessica stood up and tried to regain her composure, brushing off her clothes and gazing angrily at the stranger who was bent over with laughter. "Stop laughing, Jackass! It's not funny. You could have given me a heart attack! Look, I don't know who you are, but my dad's a cop. I don't think he would appreciate you poking around in the woods sneaking up on people."

"Oh, such brave words from one so young. I sincerely apologize if I startled you," Mathias said as he lowered his head in an manner. "I wouldn't dare harm one single hair on an angel like you." He spoke with a deep French accent; each word seemed to blend together fluidly. Mathias began to speak as he tossed the ball up into the air and caught it as it fell.

"I couldn't help but noticing your skill in handling this soccer ball. You are very talented. It's a pity that your friends should tease you like they do."

The charming manner in which he spoke had a calming affect on Jessie. The fact that she stood in the middle of the woods with a complete stranger didn't seem to matter to her for the moment. Again she heard the voice of her teacher calling out to her through the trees. Keeping her full attention on the stranger, she politely asked for her ball.

Kneeling down, Mathias slowly rolled it towards her. With a swift movement, she retrieved it, letting the momentum carry it up her leg. Bouncing it off her knee, she caught it and placed it underneath her armpit.

"Bravo! Bravo! Well done!" Mathias said as he clapped his hands together. "As I said, a talent such as yours should never be mocked. Now I suspect the voice that I keep hearing will be upon us at any moment." Jessie could hear her teacher calling out to her through the trees. "Jessie, there you are!" Sweetheart, are you ok?"

Jessica began to smile as she turned around to see her teacher standing a few paces behind her. "Yes, I'm ok! I was just talking to this man here who found my ball; he scared the crap out of me." She turned her gaze back to the spot where the stranger stood.

"Miss Price, I would like you to meet Mr.— Uh, you know what; I don't even know his name." Mathias stepped forward and introduced himself.

"Pardon me. I have such poor manners. You may call me Mathias. You have a very brave and talented student there." Miss Price walked forward so that she stood right next to Jessica and placed an arm around her. "I don't mean to be rude but what are you doing on these premises?"

Mathias looked down at the ground and smiled, he waited for a moment before answering. From his coat pocket he pulled out what looked like a dog leash. Letting it unwind to its full length, he held it outwards for them to see. "I was walking my dog through the park, a few blocks away from here, when he caught the scent of another animal. Before I could do anything to prevent it he broke loose and I followed him all the way here!"

"These grounds are considered private property owned by the school. Miss Price added, "As innocent as it may seem, you are still trespassing."

"I see. Well, I guess it would be best if I were on my way," Mathias said. "I have no wish to further offend you with my presence."

Suddenly, they heard a rustling noise coming from within the bushes and out of the foliage sprang an enormous wolf that trotted boldly right up to them. Jessica and Miss Price recoiled at the sight of the jet black wolf that glared at them intensely. It measured over six feet in length and weighed at least one hundred and eighty pounds. He trotted up towards Mathias with a dead rabbit dangling from his mouth, and then laid it down gently at his master's feet. His long, pink tongue dangled out of his mouth as he continued his forceful panting.

Jessie could see his massive chest heaving with every breath he took. He was the largest canine she had ever seen, intimidating yet impressive at the same time. Kneeling down, Mathias patted the solid flank of his companion. He spoke with a surprised tone as he ran his fingers through the thick glossy black fur.

"Drako, where have you've been, boy, it seems as though you brought me a present again?" Mathias looked up at the two astonished women and smiled, flashing his small, pointy fangs at Jessica. He started to attach the leash to the clasp on the diamond-studded collar around Drako's huge neck. Mathias continued to rub the wolf's thick fur, massaging deeply into its mane. All the while Drako looked on with watchful eyes at the two women whose hearts raced with fear.

Miss Price felt guilty for taking such a harsh tone with the stranger whose story now seemed legitimate. Showing a renewed bravery, the substitute teacher walked over slowly towards Mathias. "I apologize if I came across a bit rough towards you, but I am very protective of my students. Taking into consideration everything that has been happening lately, I mean with all the murders in the city, I'm sure you understand."

Mathias rose to his full height and edged closer towards the woman extending a gloved hand. "Think nothing of it. It has been said that regret is sometimes a wasted emotion. Besides, encountering a beauty such as yours is rare and should be handled with the utmost delicacy," Mathias said as he took her hand in his and gently kissed the top of it. He continued to pour on his charm, enchanting her with the sound of his voice and the rhythm of his words. "Let's pretend for a moment that time was ours to command. If such a thing were possible, then would you make time to spend with me?" Surprised by his boldness, Miss Price seemed to blush as she accepted his gesture.

Not knowing what to make of this situation, Jessie was dumb-founded by the spectacle. As she watched the two of them talk, she began to notice how charming Mathias was and how good he was with words. Before long, he was pulling out a notepad and jotting down Miss Price's phone number.

"Ahem!" Jessie said. "I don't mean to interrupt, but Miss Price I think I heard the bell ring. Uh Hello, Miss Price?"

Turning around towards Jessie with wide eyes, Miss Price looked at her watch then placed both hands to the side of her face in astonishment.

"Oh my God, look at the time. I hate to admit it, but Jessie is right. Within the next minute or so, I will have about twenty-five rowdy students destroying my classroom if I don't show up soon. So if you'd please excuse us, we'd better be heading back now."

She extended her hand out to his for a final handshake and he met her advance in kind and lowered his head. Slightly amused with his old fashioned courtesy, she silently cooed to herself and turned to walk away but stopped in her tracks. There was something else on her mind that she wanted to tell him.

"Um... this might sound weird but I just had the strangest feeling that you are a soccer fan. Am I right? I was thinking that maybe if you are not too busy the school has a game against North West in two days. I feel so bad for the way I acted and I'd like to make it up to you by getting you a free ticket, that is, if you are not too busy?"

Mathias appeared surprised by the woman's offer. "I shall attend only if you are there to keep me company," Mathias said.

"Oh I will be there. I wouldn't miss this for anything in the world," Miss Price answered.

"Well then, Miss Price, I guess we shall have what you Americans call a date?"

"Ashley!" She interjected. "You can just call me Ashley."

"Oh my God! I can't believe it; Miss Price is totally at this guy's mercy," Jessie thought as she looked on puzzled by her teacher's reactions.

Mathias shot a quick glance her way and smiled. "It almost seems like he can read my thoughts," Jessica mumbled beneath her breath. In that exact moment Jessica got the strangest feeling, "What if he can read people's thoughts? After all, he knew exactly what to say to have Miss Price eating out of the palm of his hands." A chill went down her spine as the eye contact shared between her and Mathias grew colder by the moment. It almost felt as though time itself slowed to a halt. Mathias was the first to break eye contact and revert back to his charming demeanor.

"Well, now that I have been reunited with my companion, we shall be on our way," Mathias said as he turned his attention back towards the woods from whence he came.

Almost as if prompted by a silent command, the wolf raised up on all fours ready to follow his master. A sensation passed through Jessica's body, chilling her to the bone as she watched Mathias walk away.

"Now that's a man, handsome, classy, and well mannered," Miss Price whispered to Jessie under her breath. "Let's get you to class before I lose my job." Warmly she smiled at Jessica and together they walked back into the school unaware of the danger that they had just faced.

Not long after Mathias and his companion disappeared into the dense forest, the beast at his side began to pulsate with a shimmering green light. Its physical shape slowly shifted from that of a canine on all fours to a young man, bent over, gradually rising to a height almost equal to Mathias. His jet black hair was pulled back into a long ponytail that went down to the middle of his back. His face was chiseled and youthful, almost beautiful; unnatural dark blue eyes surveyed the world around him through narrow slants, as if he was of oriental descent.

If asked to guess his age, one would guess him to be twenty-five years old, no more than that. He stood well above six feet; his build was athletic but not so much that would draw too much attention. Like any predator, he appeared to be sleek, intelligent, and above all capable of blending in with his environment. Drako wore form-fitted black leather trousers with a silver belt buckle.

His body length overcoat was leather as well. Beneath it, he wore a chain mail shirt with elaborately decorated glyphs interwoven into its metal. A platinum and diamond studded necklace hung loosely from his neck. Silently he eyed his surroundings, and after looking at his companion he began to smile. He didn't have to say anything. Mathias knew his thoughts all too well. A simple nod of his head illustrated his approval of the game which was about to commence.

Driven by an instinct for survival, the wildlife of the forest for miles around began to scatter as two dark immortals moved through the foliage and disappeared into the shadows.

CHAPTER 7

The Epiphany

Alone in his modestly furnished three bed room apartment, John Graham thumbed through a collection of old vinyl records. As he inspected his coveted ensemble of musical classics, a smile of satisfaction began to take form upon his face. Carefully he wiped the dust away from a cover of one his personal favorites. With one hand, he held out a copy of Led Zeppelin's *Stairway to Heaven*. To some die-hard fans, this particular album is counted, among others of that era, as a masterpiece.

To John it was without a doubt a work of art. It always seemed to remind him of better days, back to a time when music was performed live with real instruments. Unlike the artists of today whose music is dominated by artificial sounds, mimicked by high-tech synthesizers, and generated by computers.

Things were much simpler when he was young. His generation was drawn to city music auditoriums that accommodated large crowds. The combination of dazzling electric lights and smoke generators gave life to concerts back then. Gently, John removed the album out of its protective cover and placed it on the antique record player. After putting the needle on the surface of the record, he sat back in his favorite seat. Moments passed as the record began to spin. The familiar crackle of static from inaudible background noise began to pour through the ten-inch house speakers.

As the instrumental of *Stairway to Heaven* began to play, John leaned back deeper in his recliner and picked up a classic Fender electrical guitar. Positioning his hands on its strings, he began to play in unison with the music.

Stopping midway in the song, he paused and reflected back to a similar scene from his past. It was the summer of 1973, a time when Americans were attempting to recover from an unpopular and politically controversial war in Vietnam. John was only ten years old back then. His older brother Jake was drafted into the Army as an infantryman. After serving ten months in Vietnam, Jake came home to us in a casket draped with an American flag. John clearly remembered every moment as if it were yesterday.

Before he left for the war, Jake would always let John hang out with him in his room. Being the eldest of five kids, Jake never had any privacy. Their mother was a nurse's assistant who worked twelve hour shifts at Memorial Hospital. Their father worked with a big industrial construction company that helped to develop a large majority of Jersey City's modern day skyline.

Both had demanding jobs that required long hours, and they depended on Jake to keep the other children in line while they were at work. The children were Cathy, who was a year younger than John. Then there were the twins, David and Elaine, who were two of the most mischievous four year-olds ever.

When Jake had turned seventeen, he'd spent the majority of the summer helping his father in restoring the basement, which by the way, was a burdensome place. The basement occasionally flooded during the rainy seasons, but by the time they were finished, Jake had turned that place into a miniature apartment, fully equipped with a kitchenette and bathroom.

John would go down there and sit with him for hours,

listening in on the jam sessions he and a hand full of guys from the neighborhood would have. They had put together a little rock band and would play all day long during the summer. Jake was the group's lead guitarist. Everyone knew he had something special.

A few days after Jake's funeral, John remembered going down to his room. Within less than an hour of sitting on the steps, John noticed a reel of musical recordings Jake's band had put together. After listening to a few of his songs, John started to cry. At that moment, John realized that Jake was gone and would never come down those stairs again.

Nothing anyone said could ease the pain of his passing. Even to this day whenever John hears rock and roll from that time, especially Led Zeppelin's *Stairway to Heaven,* he imagines Jake playing.

John looked down at the highly polished ivory colored Fender guitar that lay within his grasp. He could vividly recall how his brother had placed it in his hands before he shipped out for boot camp. It had been in his possession ever since that day.

Before the album ended, John had slipped off into a deep sleep. Without warning, the front door opened and slammed shut. A girl ran up a flight of stairs to a room directly above his location and slammed the door.

Rudely awakened by his daughter's noisy entrance, John sat up, slowly attempting to shake off the drowsiness of his evening nap. "Jessie," he called out.

After not receiving a reply, he stood up and then stretched. Looking down at his watch, he was amazed to see that it was 15:30. A half hour had passed during his brief slumber. Barely awake, he began to walk through the apartment. In no time he closed the short distance that separated the living room from the main hall. To the left of the front door were stairs that led to the rooms above. As he drew near to the top of the stairs, he could hear muffled sounds of weeping coming from his daughter's room.

"Hello in there. Is it ok for me to come in?" John said as he leaned against the wall with his shoulder knocking gently on the door. A few moments passed, and John could hear a light shuffle of feet across the floor. Followed by the unmistakable clicking sound of the door's lock disengaging. Patiently, John stood in the hall waiting for Jessie to open the door. After a second had passed, he tapped softly upon its surface, this time speaking through the door. "Are you dressed, Jessie? Okay. I'm coming in," he said.

Slowly, he turned the knob and entered the room. On a bed filled with teddy bears lay his daughter Jessica Graham. Her room was dominated with pastel colors and curtains of pink and white lace. Scattered randomly on the walls were posters of male teen idols and various music bands. Jessica Graham lay curled up beneath her sheets, her long blonde hair was a jumbled mass. Her face was pressed deeply against plush, down-feathered pillows.

Crying softly, she spoke in a muffled voice. "I hate this place, Dad, and I hate my school!" John sat at the edge of the bed and placed his hand on her shoulder.

"What do you mean, Sweetheart? I thought you liked it here."

"Not any more," Jessie sniffled.

Carefully, using a father's finesse, John pressed forward. "Well, do you want to talk about it?"

Slowly, Jessie raised her head from her shelter of pillows and stared up at her father with red, swollen eyes. Her face was puffy from the tears she had shed.

"How long has she been crying?" John thought to himself. As they met each other's gaze, John looked at her more carefully, thoroughly inspecting her face and arms for bruises. Knowing full well his daughter's temper, John contemplated the idea that she might have had an altercation with another student. He couldn't help but see how much she resembled her mother.

"The only thing she seems to have gotten from me is my temper and stubborn disposition," John thought. As John stared into his daughter's eyes, he saw for a brief moment her mother looking back at him.

"Go ahead, Jessie," John said, "I'm listening. What happened today?"

Slowly, Jessie sat up against the headboard, propping her knees up to her chest. She carefully wiped the tears away from her eyes and looked over towards a picture that sat on her nightstand. It was a photo that was taken when she was five years old. In it she sat smiling on the shoulders of her father. A beautiful woman with long blond hair stood next to them on her tip toes attempting to kiss her on the cheek.

Jessie thought to herself that she must have looked at this picture at least a million times, and each time she'd lose herself in every detail. This time Jessie saw something different. She noticed that her tiny hands were wrapped around her father's face, covering his eyes. In the background, a huge roller coaster and Ferris wheel sat in the distance. To their left ran the length of a pier. Behind the rail lay the vastness of the Atlantic Ocean which spread out towards the horizon. "That was one of the happiest days of my life," Jessie thought to herself. Grabbing the picture of her family, she pressed it tightly to her breast.

"I miss her," Jessie whispered.

"I know you do, Sweetheart," John replied. "I miss her too!"

For a brief moment they embraced one another, attempting to comfort a deep pain they both shared. For one, it was the death of a wife and companion; for the other, it was the irreplaceable loss of a mother.

"I wish she were here. Why did she have to die?" Jessie said as she began to weep, fiercely burying her head within her father's chest.

No words came from John's mouth because inside his mind burned the very same question. He was no stranger to losing those who were close to him. If there was a God in Heaven, only he would know the reasons why. Long ago, his faith was lost to him. He no longer believed in the idealism of a divine scheme, where one all-powerful being controlled the balance of lives. It was exactly one year after they had taken that picture that his wife Susan was murdered.

Jessie said beneath her breath, "If Mom were here, she'd know how to handle the girls at school."

Feeling a little defeated, John paused and meditated on her words. "I know it's tough right now, Kid-o. Just hang in there a little longer. Give your self some time. I'm sure things will turn out just fine." John looked at his daughter and attempted to make her smile. With a nudge, he tugged at her shoulder, adding, "Besides, you made the soccer team, right? It's only a matter of time before you are on the starting line up, dazzling the crowd with the moves I taught you." Jessie looked up at her father sarcastically. Forgetting her despair, she replied, "Moves you taught me. Yeah right, Dad."

For a brief moment all of the painful memories shared between them no longer seemed to matter. It was as if the heavy weight that burdened him for so long had been lifted. It is said that time has the ability to heal all wounds, regardless of how deep they may be. For John and Jessica Graham, hope was a certainty that lay over the horizon. However, there was something else that lingered in the distance, a being, ancient and menacing, shrouded within an unnatural shadowy mist. For some time it had lingered there, totally unseen by mortal eyes. By a sheer act of will, its thoughts has probed into their home, and like a thief in the night it peered into the windows of their minds, making their most sacred thoughts known to him. Calling upon the dark powers that were his to command, Mathias pulled away the veil and took on the mortal guise that fancied him the most. Tall with broad shoulders, he stood; his long blonde hair was pulled back neatly and fell midway down his back.

With slow and methodical movements his preternatural eyes scanned the surrounding area. As he glanced towards the horizon, Mathias could see that the sun had begun to descend along its celestial arc, setting swiftly in the west. Its radiance was fading slowly behind darkening rain clouds which filled the sky with shades of deep violet and orange. Mathias' thoughts were bent solely upon that which he relished most. He had chosen his prey and it was almost within his grasp.

There was nothing he coveted more than twisting pure souls to do his will. He had endured a thousand lifetimes purely for the thrill of the hunt and the inevitable kill. Mathias paused as his keen sense of smell caught a familiar scent which had been carried by a northern breeze. Instinctively, he knew what was in pursuit. Nevertheless, he would be long gone before it would arrive. t would be nightfall soon, and he would feed upon human blood until he had his fill.

Taking one last look at the home of John and Jessica Graham, Mathias knew there would be another time to continue his game. This would only be a momentary reprieve for his quarry. Effortlessly, Mathias willed his physical form to shift into mist. Then he vanished into the shadows, embracing the emptiness of the approaching night.

CHAPTER 8

Convergence

Victor awoke from his sleep feeling well rested and invigorated. The night had passed by without incident. There were no dark and menacing visions which came to haunt his dreams. In fact, he didn't remember dreaming at all. It was a quarter past nine and the light of the morning sun blazed through his window. Victor got up slowly from his bed and began to stretch upwards; he was amazed to see that his long and slender hands nearly touched the ceiling.

Being only five foot eleven, he was not exceptionally tall, not in this day and age. When this chateau was built nearly one thousand years ago, that probably would have been true. In any case, he could feel the blood beginning to flow to the parts of his body that were still numb from his rest. As he walked towards the window, Victor could feel the heat of the suns rays on his face and arms. Sliding back a latch, he opened the window and marveled at all the smells that filled his nostrils as he drew in a deep breath.

All of the prominent signs of fall were in the air. A cool breeze carried the aroma of acorns which lay in heaps beneath the trees below. Victor closed his eyes for a moment and listened to the sway of the trees as the wind filled their branches, "This is it,"

Victor thought to himself, "and this is what life is all about." The experience as a whole was invigorating to him, yet there were other smells that caught his attention. It was the fragrance of freshly baked bread mingled with the unmistakable odor of dried sausages that entered his nostrils.

Almost instantly, Victor's stomach began to growl in response to his hunger. Immediately, he went to his bathroom and prepared a warm shower. Then he went to a walk-in closet and pulled out a set of garments for the day; a freshly pressed long-sleeved cotton shirt, an oxford styled knitted sweater, and a pair of slacks. Satisfied with the ensemble that he had selected, Victor walked towards the steaming shower that awaited him.

Two forceful knocks at the door caused him to stop completely in his tracks and head for the door. Before he was able to unbolt the latch, two additional and even more urgent raps followed the first set of blows. As he opened the door, Victor found himself looking his mentor squarely in the eye. Edward did not wait for any formal greeting from his apprentice. Instead, he let himself into the room. Always true to his normal demeanor, he carried himself as the dignified English gentleman, walking past Victor with his head high, chest out, and his arms placed behind his back.

"I trust that you were able to keep the particulars of our most recent communication secure from all others as I charged you to do?" Edward said.

"No one knows anything we spoke of master. Of this I am certain," Victor replied as he stepped aside and closed the door the door behind him. Edward had begun to walk around the room looking inquisitively in every direction. Every now and then, he would pick up an item at random and hold it up to the light in order to get a better view. Once his curiosity was satisfied with the trinkets in his hand, he would place them back in the spot from whence they came. Edward stood with his back turned to his young apprentice; he was looking up at an oil painting that Victor had made. It was a landscape portrait of a hilltop, filled with olive trees and a vast vineyard that spread out towards a setting sun.

"Your skill has definitely improved over the years, Victor," Edward said as he extended a finger lightly tracing the contours of the painting. He was amazed at the detail placed in his pupil's work, especially the way each of the colors blended perfectly with one another upon the canvas.

Victor could barely stand the nonchalant performance his master was putting on. Edwards's reluctant behavior and his use of stall tactics pushed Victor well beyond his limits. "What news of the Inner Council, Master?" Victor said as he approached his mentor.

Slowly, Edward turned around to face the young man who looked at him with ever growing anticipation. Edward didn't answer him immediately. Instead, he reached into the inside pocket of his jacket and pulled out two plane tickets.

"You might want to pack warmly lad. I'm afraid the east coast of the United States is dreadfully unpredictable this time of year." A smile appeared on Victor's face as he raced to his closet and grabbed a set of luggage.

Edward had settled back into a chair and pulled out a wooden pipe and a pouch filled with his favorite imported tobacco. After filling his pipe, Edward pulled out a match to light the contents. Normally, Victor was repulsed by the repugnant odor made by cigarette smoke; however, he didn't mind the sweet vanilla aroma that Edward's tobacco gave off. Victor glanced over at his mentor who lounged in a chair nonchalantly gazing at his apprentice's newly created work of art; his lips were pursed around the reed stock of his horn shaped pipe.

He took in deep breaths and forced the smoke to flow from his nostrils down into his thick beard. Twice the pipe had extinguished itself, and twice Edward retrieved a match from his pocket to rekindle the cinders until the tobacco was burning independently.

With each puff from Edward's pipe, the room began to fill with the sweet aroma of vanilla. Light clouds of smoke rose in wisps and flowed listlessly about, carried by a cool fall breeze. Edward appeared to be calm and content as he sat with one leg crossed over the other, watching his young apprentice with amusement as he dashed about the room grabbing his personal belongings.

Edward began to talk in a slow yet continuous flow of words, filling Victor in on the specifics of their journey. For more than just personal or professional reasons, he chose to omit certain details of his discussions with the Illuminate's secretive inner council.

Within hours they had both eaten and made their final preparations, their bags were loaded into the back of Edward's personal limousine and they were driven away. No goodbyes were said to either one of their associates. In fact, no one was allowed to know the nature of this venture. As they passed through the towering gates of the Illuminate Mother house, Victor turned around to look at the place he has called his home for the last sixteen years. Something deep within his heart gave him the feeling as if this farewell would possibly be for the last time.

Part II *Convergence*
BAD OMEN

Timeline: Tuesday, October 5th 4:30 p.m.
Eastern Standard Time
Location: A middleclass Jersey City suburb

"**P**lease hurry, Dad, or I'm going to be late for my game!" Jessica Graham said as she ran frantically down a flight of stairs towards the front door of her home. She wore a red and white striped soccer jersey, black on black-checkered knee length shorts, and a pair of cleats, which hung by their laces around her shoulders.

"Coach Harris said that if anyone is late for pre game warm-up they'll be benched for the entire game, so please hurry!"

"Ok already. I'll be there in a minute," John said as he examined himself in the bathroom mirror. "Great! I just cut myself shaving!" He winched slightly in pain as he pulled away a napkin revealing an inch-long gash beneath his throat

"Jessie, do me a favor and start the car. The keys should be on the kitchen counter where I left them." John walked back into the bathroom and grabbed another handful of napkins, discarding the bloody one that was pressed against his neck.

Jessie sighed impatiently then went to retrieve the set of keys that were on a counter in the kitchen. After grabbing them, she headed outside to the burgundy colored Chevy Lumina that was parked in the driveway. This was the most important game of the season, and it seemed like her father was more nervous than she was, Jessie thought to herself as she opened the driver's-side door and slid down comfortably into the plush grey colored leather interior. After she inserted the key and turned the ignition, the engine roared to life.

She seemed to marvel at the deep guttural sound that came from beneath the hood. As she settled back into the driver's seat, Jessie smiled wickedly as she playfully pressed on the gas. She reached down at a console and turned the knob on the sound system. Instantly, loud music poured out of the speakers. Jessica started to dance in the seat, bobbing her head up and down throwing her hands up in the air. For a moment she was caught up in the energy of the song.

A tap against the window brought her out of her daze. Looking up and over her left shoulder, Jessie saw her father standing outside the window looking down at her shaking his head. His mouth was moving but she couldn't hear his words. He motioned with his hands for her to turn the volume down.

Playfully, she pressed a hand to her ear pretending to not be able to hear.

"Huh? What? Did you say something? You need to speak up, Dad, I can't hear you." John peered down at his daughter with a straight face and crossed his arms. Jessie looked at him and exploded into laughter.

John held up his left hand pointing to his watch and said, "We don't have time for this, Jessie, now slide over." In silent response, Jessie poked her lips out, unlocked the door, and slid over into the passenger seat.

"What the hell are you listening to anyway, Jessie?" John said as he climbed into the car turning down the volume.

"Little John and the Ying Yang Twins," Jessica replied reaching back over to turn the volume up again.

"Little Who, With the What"? John said sarcastically as he turned the volume down again, this time changing the channel altogether. The radio had a pre-set station that played his favorite classic rock. "Now this is music kid, not that bee-bop junk you were just listening to."

"It's called Hip Hop, Dad, and it's not junk. Sometimes you can be so lame," Jessie replied as she folded her arms across her chest and turning her head so she could look out her window. As their car edged out of the driveway, she saw a man standing on the sidewalk directly across the street from her house. He made no sudden movements, only stood absolutely still glancing down at the ground. It appeared as though he was examining the area as if he were searching for something. In a physical sense he reminded her of the man she encountered in the woods behind her school the other day. Outwardly, he seemed more humble and sort of homely; his clothing was faded and weather-beaten as if he spent many nights under makeshift shelters. He looked up for a moment and placed his hands in the pockets of his trench coat and stared at her from across the distance with the most peculiar expressions. Their eyes met for a brief moment, this proved to be more than enough time for Raziel to peel away the fragile barriers of her mind.

"Yield your thoughts to me!" Raziel said as his telepathic powers reached out to her from across the distance which separated them. In response to his call, random images flowed into his mind like water. A myriad of images flashed before him; all of the things she held secure away from the world were laid bare before him. Within a fraction of a second, Raziel knew what she knew and saw what she had seen. Raziel kept only the things which he needed and discarded the rest.

In most cases there would be nothing of any great importance that would be revealed to him. Over the centuries his quarry has become increasingly clever in concealing their clandestine activities and covering their tracks. However, this time was different because it was the unmistakable visage of an immortal he saw that caused his spirit to quicken. Despite its deceptive disguise, Raziel knew this being for what it was.

It bore the same physical similarities he possessed and contained all of the preternatural proportions that were emblazoned clearly upon his face. Raziel was momentarily puzzled. So much was this confusion that he began to second guess himself. Was it not the very same dark essence which he tracked from the city that led him to this exact spot? Even now to see the face of one of his kind through the mind of this mortal child caused even more questions to build within him. There is no way he could have been mistaken by this vision. It is not entirely impossible that he was not the only immortal attracted to the pull of the demon he pursued. There was no doubt that he had traced the dark essence from the city to this exact location.

Raziel continued to look around and could detect faint traces of this menacing energy lingering in the bushes and in every blade of grass that the foul creature had touched. As the car disappeared down the street among the light traffic of commuters passing by, Raziel pondered even more deeply.

Now he focused his thoughts back to the child who had come into contact with one of his kind. Again came the overwhelming sense of confusion that lingered in his mind. Never before had he been so unsure of his abilities to see through illusions, yet now he could not ascertain the true nature of the being whose face he saw so clearly. There were few of the fallen left who were powerful enough to cloak themselves in such a fashion.

Whether fallen angel or a comrade drawn by the dark pull, Raziel was now aware of this being. Without the slightest thought, Raziel willed himself into the air and took flight, continuing the pursuit of his elusive, immortal enemy.

Within minutes, John and Jessica Graham arrived at their destination. The sports stadium of the middle school was half packed to capacity with students and family members who sat waiting for the soccer game to start. Once her father had parked, Jessie got out of the car and ran to join her teammates who were in a circle doing stretching exercises. Stopping at a bench on the sideline, she swiftly removed her shoes and put on her cleats. Carrying a clipboard, a short, stubby woman in her thirties came up to her.

The woman was wearing a sporty windbreaker jacket with the same colors as Jessie's jersey. Her light brown hair was cut short in a bob and hung above her shoulders.

"Cutting it close, Graham," She said as she looked down at Jessie. "I'm putting you in at right guard. Sarah Hanson just sprang her ankle no more than five minutes ago. She turned and pointed at a slender redhead girl with freckles, the very same girl that had taunted Jessie the other day.

"I can imagine the pain your heart is feeling for her right now," Coach Harris said sarcastically looking down at Jessie over the rim of her glasses. "You've been kicking butt in practice lately, showing me that you really want to play. So here's your chance to impress me. If you do, then the slot is yours …permanently."

Jessie looked up at her coach and smiled, then glanced over at her antagonistic teammate who sat in the bleachers glaring down at her with tears of hate and in her eyes. A warm hand on her shoulders turned her attention away from the disgruntled redhead. Her father bent down and kissed her on top of her head and said, "Make me proud, Kiddo. I know you're going to do great. Win, lose, or draw, I'm still your biggest fan!" After giving his daughter those words of encouragement, John walked off and found a seat in the bleachers two rows away from her.

Jessie ran down to join her teammates on the field. The air was crisp and the sun had already begun to set in the west. Before it had completely faded away, the lights of the stadium were turned on, illuminating the surrounding area. As the team captains from both sides came out to the center of the field and shook hands, there was a coin toss which determined that New Providence Middle School would have possession of the ball. The tension that lingered in the air came to an abrupt end when the head official's whistle set the game into motion. The air was filled with cheers from both the home and visitor sections of the stadium.

Jessie ran onto the field and took her position. Her heart pounded with excitement. She could feel her hands and legs tremble, not from fear but from the anticipation to perform. A teammate who was in the center position passed the ball to her on the initial kick off, and she dribbled it forward with expert skill and precision. An opponent advanced in on her attempting to take the ball. Jessie picked up her pace and out-sprinted her adversary.

The spectators in the stand were in frenzy, some dazzled by her display of dominance, others shouted out heckles at the opposing team who pursued her. Jessie seemed at ease on the field, and early in the game, she seemed to take the momentum of the game up a notch.

Two teammates rallied behind her, and she passed the ball to a girl positioned on her left. The opposing team shifted and took on a more defensive formation, creating a semi-circular wall around them. Control of the ball shifted back and forth between the rival teams.

Within seconds, Jessie and her teammates moved within scoring range of the opposing team's goal. All eyes were fixed on the field and the ball as it moved across the field and into Jessie's skillful possession. She pressed forward with the ball as if it were an extension of her body.

Once within fifty feet of the goal, she locked eyes with the goalie who was bent over with both hands held out, poised and ready to deflect the kick. It was the scenario Jessie had imagined in her mind at least a thousand times. Her heart pounded fiercely and her throat burned from her exertions. Everything around Jessie was a blur even the seconds on the time clock took infinity to pass. Jessie focused on her objective. As she drew back to kick, an opponent sideswiped her from the left, causing her to fall violently to the ground. Immediately a whistle blew and a referee threw a yellow penalty card. A wave of boos came from the stands in response to the display of un-sportsmanlike conduct.

Jessie stood up and wiped off a clump of grass and dirt that had stuck to her knee. She was fouled within the penalty area, and as a result she was to receive a free shot at the goal. The referee walked over to her and asked if she was ok. She nodded her head up and down. He then handed her the ball and led her to the spot on the ground where she was to place it.

"This is my chance to put a score on the board for the team," Jessie told herself. The spectators for the opposing team were on their feet yelling out attempting to throw off her concentration. She hesitated for a moment and looked over to the stand where her father was seated. She found him immediately. He was also on his feet, smiling and clapping his hands together. He whistled loudly and shouted words of encouragement to his daughter as he gave her the thumbs up sign.

A few rows behind him sat Miss Price who was clearly preoccupied and paid very little attention to the game. She was snuggled up next to a man dressed in an overcoat and business suit. He sat upright in his seat with one leg crossed over the other.

Jessie recognized him immediately. It was Mathias, the man whom she encountered in the woods two days prior. Everything about him was the same except for his lustrous blonde hair that was now parted down the middle and hung freely down his shoulders.

He peered at her from behind a pair of lightly tinted blue glasses. His gaze remained intense and was fixed upon her every movement. He seemed totally disinterested with the young woman who sat beside him. Occasionally he would push away her wandering hands that groped incessantly at his thick and muscular legs. The woman's displays of affection meant nothing to him. Mathias was a bit annoyed with the situation, but he allowed her to lavish him with her sexual advances. This was nothing more than a game to him, a role which he played to seem as normal as any other man. He used the woman at his side as a shield which would allow him access to his true prize.

His handsome features turned the heads of several women who immediately took notice of him. Even some of the men close by took a second and sometimes even a third glance at the stranger who became the center of attention. Slowly, he removed his glasses, and his eyes connected directly with Jessie's. The lights of the stadium gave his emerald green eyes an eerie appearance, causing them to seem to shimmer in the night.

The hairs on her arms rose, and her flesh seemed to crawl in reaction to the momentary connection with Mathias. Jessie felt a tug on her shoulder and she was drawn immediately back into the present. She found herself lying on the ground with her coach and the team physician kneeling over her checking her head for bruises. It was apparent that she had blacked out from the impact of her collision with the other player.

Everything that had happened before she found herself in this current condition seemed so real. Yet immediately when she looked over to the bleachers searching for Mathias, neither he nor Miss Price were anywhere to be found. The spot where the two had been seated was occupied by a handful of school kids who looked on enthusiastically at the spectacle transpiring on the field.

Jessica was absolutely disorientated. She stood up and attempted to regain her focus. For the sake of her sanity, she chose to accept the possibility of being rendered unconscious. The official who had been close by asked if she was ok. He looked her over with a raised brow. Satisfied that she was coherent and able to continue, he led her to the spot where she was to take her foul shot. After handing her the ball, the official blew his whistle bringing the game back into play. Jessie hesitated for a moment and scanned her surroundings one last time before squaring off on the ball at her feet. After taking several deep breaths, she took two steps backwards, paused, then ran and struck the ball with all of her might.

She sent it sailing inches above the ground, straight towards the net. The goalie leapt outwards with both arms fully extended attempting to deflect the ball. A streak of black and white leather soared by the goal keeper and found its mark. The home team was on their feet and the crowd went wild with excitement.

As the game continued on, the score was now tied at three points a piece. The momentum of the event was at an all time high as the two teams played with equal levels of determination. Two minutes remained in the game when Jessica scored the final point which resulted in her team's victory over their longtime rival. An official ran out to the middle of the soccer field waving his hands and blowing his whistle signifying the conclusion of the game.

The prep school North East, who had dominated them for the last five years, had finally been beaten. The remaining teammates who stood on the sidelines rushed onto the field celebrating their long overdue victory. Some headed straight for Jessie and raised her high upon their shoulders carrying her to center field. Tonight was definitely one to remember Jessie thought to her self as she looked down to see her coach standing outside the ring of players who held her above their heads. The woman was holding the game ball in her right palm.

"Enough already! Let's get it together for a minute, ladies!" she said in an authoritative tone. Despite her short, squat appearance, Coach Harris spoke loudly enough to be heard above the ecstatic girls who were jumping up and down and hugging one another in excitement. The ruckus died down, and Jessie was lowered to the ground before the woman continued to speak. She looked around and began to counting all of her players.

"I have fourteen bodies here ladies and I'm still missing one. Who's not here?" Coach Harris said as she looked around. A girl pointed over to the bleachers at Sarah Hansen who was hobbling off on her crutches away from the field.

"Hey! Where do you think you are going Hansen?" Last time I checked you are still part of this team, broken ankle or not."

Sarah stopped dead in her tracks, lowered her head, and turned back to join the rest of the group. Jessie could tell by the expression on her face that she was salty and didn't want anything to do with this little fiasco. Up until this evening Sarah had been the star of the team. Today Jessie was able to show exactly what she could do, and the result was a victory. Once Sarah took her place among the circle of girls who surrounded their coach, she looked over at Jessie, giving her a look filled with resentment.

"Good of you to join us," Coach Harris said sarcastically to the red haired girl who was flushed both with anger and embarrassment. Sporadic giggles erupted from two girls who at one time hung out with Sarah.

Jessie's head began to spin as she noticed how swiftly the roles had shifted in her favor. She now seemed to have secured a position with the popular in-crowd. The entire time Coach Harris gave her victory speech, Jessie stood in a daze. As she looked around, Jessie started to reflect on the chain of events. The entire experience was a little overwhelming at first, but as she looked over at Sarah Hansen, deep down inside, she knew that justice was being served.

Despite how cruel it may have been to see Sarah humiliated by her former sidekicks, Jessie felt no pity for her whatsoever. The more the girls poked fun at Sarah, the more Jessie relished this feeling that swelled inside her.

"So in conclusion, I want to present the game ball to Jessica Graham... Good job, kid, way to step up!" Coach Harris finished her speech and tossed Jessie the soccer ball. Loud whistles and a round of applause followed her gesture. Someone in the circle yelled out the word *speech*. Others followed the request, and Jessie turned red with embarrassment. She couldn't find the words to say, and when she was about to speak she felt an eerie sensation flowing down her spine that caused the hairs on the back of her neck to rise. Instinctively, she looked towards the edge of the woods where she ventured into the other day.

She saw a tall figure leaning against a tree with his arms folded across his chest. It was Mathias who peered at her from across the distance. He wore the exact same garments she had seen him in during the game. "This can't be," Jessie said to herself. Up to this point, she had convinced herself that she had imagined the whole thing. Yet there he was plain as day standing beneath the trees, his emerald green eyes illuminating in the darkness. Her momentary stupor was interrupted by a voice that called out to her.

"What are you looking for over there, Hotshot?" Coach Harris asked as she turned to look in the direction Jessie's gaze had been locked on. Jessie turned her attention back to the group who looked up at her confused by her strange behavior. She looked back in the direction where Mathias had been standing only to find an empty spot. There was no way she was going to spoil her moment of glory by trying to explain a guy that kept popping in and out on her. She turned back to the group and paused for a second before answering her coach.

"Nothing," she said. I wasn't looking at anything in particular, just trying to find the right words to say. I'll keep it short by saying that this ball is belongs to the team. There's no way that I could have done it by myself."

The team gave another round of applause, and Coach Harris nodded her head in approval. She added a few more words of encouragement and even touched on some areas that she thought they needed to improve on as a whole. After the team had gathered together and said their motto, they were released to their families who waited patiently on the sidelines.

Jessie walked over to her father who stood by the bleachers smiling from ear to ear.

"Not bad; not bad at all, Kiddo. You looked pretty good out there, not as good as me in my day, but you're getting there," John said, being cute.

"Whatever, Dad!" Jessie replied as she looked up at her father and smiled. As they made their way across the empty parking lot, she continued to reflect upon the random thoughts that passed in her mind. It had been a long time since she remembered ever feeling this complete. "Things were finally starting to work out," She thought.

Once inside the car, Jessie retrieved a round leather case from beneath her seat. She opened the case which contained a collection of musical CD's. Within a few seconds of thumbing through her ensemble, she leaned over and placed a CD in the player. Swiftly she pressed a button on a control panel and scrolled through a set of numbers in search for a particular song. Instantly, a loud flow of music filled with ear-shattering, heart-murmuring bass pounded through the speakers.

John jumped up in his seat with his right hand pressed against his chest in total surprise at the sudden noise. He looked over at Jessie who settled deeply into her seat and hunched her shoulders up apologetically at him.

She gave her father one of the most innocent looks he had ever seen. For a moment John held his hands cupped over both ears and grimaced in pain as if his ear drums were about to explode. As he reached out towards the sound system, Jessie looked at him sharply and turned away shaking her head in disbelief. John paused for a second and before allowing himself to act upon his immediate impulse. This was the very thing that the dreaded Graham family silent treatments were made of, and he knew it.

He couldn't stand it when his wife used to employ this tactic whenever they had a disagreement, but John hated to have to deal with it from Jessie. To her surprise, John did the exact opposite of what she expected him to do; instead of turning the radio off, he turned the volume down to a more tolerable level. In utter surprise, Jessie turned in her seat to face her father and smiled then started to sing along with the music. John began to playfully mimic her movements; the automobile seemed to rock up and down as Jessica danced in her seat.

"It seems as though Dad was right. Maybe my life might be taking a change for the better after all," Jessie thought herself as she glanced at her reflection in the mirror.

Before she could ponder her thoughts any further, an animal sprang out from the thick foliage which ran along both sides of the highway. Instead of darting across the road and away from danger, it stopped dead in its tracks in the middle of the road. Time seemed to stand still as the events that followed flowed in slow motion. The animal's eyes shimmered with an eerie green luminescence as they reflected the headlights of the automobile. A silent connection seemed to have been established between Jessie and the beast as its gaze met hers.

Her father slammed on the brakes and turned the steering wheel hard to the right to avoid the collision. John's heart pounded as the adrenaline rushed through his body. It was as if he was witnessing this entire scene in slow motion as he looked over at his daughter who screamed as she held out both hands towards the dashboard. As Jessie braced herself for impact, he could hear a loud explosion from his right front tire as it ran over a jagged object which had been left among debris scattered alongside the gravel shouldered road. The night seemed to swallow them whole as the vehicle swerved uncontrollably until it flew into the wood line and down into a dark abysmal depth towards a steep embankment where an uncertain fate awaited below.

CHAPTER 9

Chasing Devils

At 6:45 p.m., the landing gear of a United Airline Boeing 747 from Rome, Italy touched down gently on a wet flight line. Within seconds after landing, the aircraft's powerful engines died down slightly, but provided enough power to propel the vessel forward, as it began to taxi across the busy airport enroute for its docking gate. The nine and a half hour international flight seemed to pass by faster than Victor had expected. He was only a child the last time he had flown, and much of the sensations he recalled back then had been dulled over the passage of time.

The journey across the Atlantic proved to be more than adequate in reacquainting him with the same nauseating sensations he felt years ago. If there was ever any doubt in his mind or a question in terms of what mode of transportation he preferred, air travel would definitely be at the bottom of the list. From the rapid climb into the heavens at a forty-five degree angle, to gut-wrenching drops in altitude thirty thousand feet above the earth's surface, all of these things proved to be more than Victor was willing to bear. Despite all of the negative aspects of the flight, it was a relief to finally hear the familiar and reassuring sound of rubber striking

105

pavement as the aircraft landed and made its way to the unloading dock.

Edward had sat upright in the seat beside him and pulled away a complimentary blanket which had been given to him by an extremely attractive female flight attendant who tended to his every whim during the entire trip. He stretched out his arms and yawned deeply, all the while looking as if he had just experienced the most peaceful sleep he'd had in years. After recovering a jacket which was slung over his armrest, he pulled out his pair of specks from an inside pocket.

Edward unfolded a thick wad of fabric which he used to safeguard his glasses from harm. After a thorough cleaning and inspection of his eyewear, he placed them on the bridge of his nose. "It's quite obvious that you did not take my advice and get some sleep," Edward said as he looked over at his young and weary-eyed apprentice. Victor's silent response confirmed his master's assumptions. It was clear that the excitement and anticipation of the journey had not allowed him to rest. Going over their mission repeatedly, he'd been awake during the entire flight. Perfection and attention to detail was two things that Edward demanded and reinforced in all his pupils. Despite his being overwhelmed by fatigue, Victor sought to suppress his primal need for sleep. By simulating sleep deprivation, to him this was an exercise meant to condition his mind to focus and remain sharp.

Edward thought back to when he took Victor into his care all those years ago. He was nothing more than a frightened child who was being tormented by his psychic abilities. To look at him now, he knew that the boy's skill would develop to a level which would surpass anyone he ever instructed within the Order, to include some of the powers the elders possessed. In truth, he had never seen an individual whose abilities were so developed at such a young age. It would take a lifetime to figure out the range of his abilities and know their limitations.

Aside from these thoughts, Edward also knew the impact that he had in Victor's life. He'd practically been like a father to him. After all, it was he who took him from a world filled with fear and neglect to another life dominated by ancient knowledge and mysticism. Now once more, he realized that his lifelong obsession has been passed on to his pupil, and they were drawing nearer to the questions which had eluded him for so long.

Victor made it a point to familiarize himself with the bits of information Edward entrusted him with. He focused primarily on the name and description of the contact that was to meet them at the terminal upon their arrival. He knew that Edward had every intention of treating this operation as if it were a mission sanctioned by the Illuminate. All the necessary preparations were made prior to their departure. Edwards's first order of business was in the appointment of a liaison, one who was familiar with the area of operations and would serve them well throughout the course of their investigation. He chose a rather scrupulous individual, one whom he had known for years and trusted above any unofficial contact he had outside the order.

Their agent was an elderly man of Greek decent named Joseph Palademos. Edward had been extremely vague in giving the exact details of how he and his Greek constituent became acquainted. He made it clear that Joseph was a very crafty and street wise individual who, despite his lack of psychic abilities or extensive knowledge of the supernatural world, was extremely resourceful and could be counted on when situations got unpleasant.

Whereas so many times agents of the Illuminate relied on their uncanny abilities to read minds and influence others to do their wills that it crippled them or made them careless over the years, Joseph, however, had no such handicaps. He utilized the more conventional methods of networking and enterprise, which proved to be just as effective. For over fifty years, he had been known and respected as a member of underground conglomerates which fueled and supported many of the political engines that exist in cities along the East Coast. Many government officials in his area received their push into seats of power from decisions which he had had input on. The connections and influences he had with key people of authority had served him well.

Being under his protection would allow them movement around the city, unchallenged by official and unofficial circles. In addition to personnel, acquisition Edward spared no expense in ensuring that the highest level of discretion was maintained. Like several times in the past, he was forced to use his own personal resources to fund an operation that the inner council had dismissed. Everything they could possibly need would be at their disposal.

Despite his meek and modest appearance, Edward Wiltshire was still without a doubt an extremely wealthy man. A large part of his wealth had stemmed from his birth into nobility, which he traced back to feudal times. Above any title he may have inherited, he held the position as chairman over a multi-billion dollar corporation, which had been passed down to him by his predecessors.

Victor had observed his mentor several times during their journey. To him, Edward had no equal when it came to concealing emotion. Despite his efforts to control his outward demeanor, however, it was evident that he was clearly on edge. "Master Wiltshire has every reason to be a bit uneasy," Victor thought as he forced himself to concentrate on the more important details of their mission. It was clear that they would be operating outside the authority and approval of the inner council. Depending on the outcome of their findings, it could either elevate or fracture their hard earned credibility within the order.

The young apprentice shuddered at his thoughts of self doubt. His instincts, along with the visions he'd been having, confirmed that they were close to uncovering something big. "There's a large amount of unnatural energy amiss," Victor thought as he sat back in his chair reaching out beyond the confines of the aircraft with his abilities.

He could feel the faint traces of the dark energies which collected in the air like static electricity, causing the hair on his arms to rise. Victor was trained to use his empathic abilities like a compass. With a certain level of accuracy, he could pinpoint this source of the dark power which he sensed. Startled by a large electronic pinging noise followed by a female voice which came over the cabin intercom, he sat up slightly. The plane had successfully docked, and specifically for passengers who had connecting flights, a flight attendant made a rapid string of announcements. People were on their feet opening the overhead compartments, retrieving their personal belongings.

It wasn't long before the two of them were standing outside the terminal. Edward pulled out a pocket watch from his blazer to check the time. It was half past seven, and the sun had already fallen into the western sky. The night air was cool, and a myriad of sounds blended together all around them. Within minutes, a black limousine pulled up and stopped directly where they stood. Immediately, a tall, well-built young man wearing glasses and a dark tailor-made suit exited the passenger side of vehicle. He didn't say a word to either one of them; instead, he walked with measured steps along the length of the vehicle and stood by the right rear door. Simultaneously, a second man exited the vehicle from the opposite side and took up a similar posture beside him.

Judging by their demeanor and the obvious bulges in their jackets, it was safe to assume that they were bodyguards for a person of wealth and importance. One of the guards reached down and opened the car door. In one fluid motion, a man emerged from the vehicle. His dark features immediately gave away his Aegean lineage; he was a rather robust fellow who stood a little over six feet tall. Dark curly brown locks covered his head; only the lightest traces of grey could be found intermingled within his trimmed goatee. Victor could see that this man was fearless, yet someone who exercised caution at all times. He had the natural look of a survivor in his eyes.

Even in the company of friends, he remained vigilant and conscious of his surroundings. Even though it would have taken little effort for Victor to scan the mind of their host, he decided against it because it would have been rude to violate a man whom Edward regarded with such respect. He focused back to Edward's account of the man who stood before them. He remembered Edward describing Joseph as an old acquaintance. Apparently, he took his master's words far too literally. Victor was expecting to be greeted by someone a little more limited and closer to his dotage. The man recognized Edward immediately, and he walked up to him in the old style of greeting, grabbing Edward by the shoulders and planting a kiss on each cheek. More words were exchanged in Greek dialect, and the two men embraced one another as brothers.

"It's been far too long, Old Friend," Joseph said as he stepped back looking Edward over more thoroughly. "You haven't changed a bit. How long has it been? Twenty, no thirty years now?"

Looking over at Victor, he said, "This must be the young man that you have spoken so highly of."

Edward stepped forward anxiously and cleared his throat, yet spoke softly as he interrupted his friend in mid sentence.

"Joseph, please forgive me if I seem a bit prudent. There is much to be discussed that is far too sensitive for our present surroundings, I'd prefer we leave this place immediately, and there will be ample time for proper introductions." Joseph looked a bit confused at Edward's directness, it was apparent that he too had never seen this side of his old friend.

"My apology, Old Friend. As always, you are right. We should be on our way now. Everything that you have requested is awaiting you," Joseph said as he looked over at his guards motioning to them. Without delay, his men sprang into action, grabbing luggage and placing them in the trunk of the limo.

Joseph stepped aside; and with an extended arm, he beckoned Edward and Victor towards the vehicle. Within seconds everyone was seated and the limousine pulled off smoothly into the night. At this point the overall mood was a bit awkward for everyone; however, Joseph sat across from his guest in silence yet forced a smile upon his face. Victor could see that inside he pondered the reasons behind Edward's use of discretion. It hadn't dawned on him before, but Victor knew with absolute certainty that Joseph was totally in the dark about the entire situation.

Edward had not yet revealed to him their reasons for being there, nor had he told Joseph what role he was to play in this. As their transport merged onto the busy turnpike, Victor turned to look out through tinted windows to see a skyline dominated by colossal buildings and structures which seemed to spread out across the horizon. Despite being awestruck by this spectacle, his experience was dampened by the obvious feeling of dread which lingered in the air. The closer they drew to the city, the stronger and more potent this feeling became.

CHAPTER 10
The Abduction

As he fought hard at the steering wheel trying to maintain control of the vehicle, John became frantic. As the car plunged headlong into the darkness, he continually pumped at the brakes, attempting to slow their descent. Despite his efforts, the automobile's brakes had locked under the strain that had been placed upon them. In an instant, random images of recent past events flashed before his eyes. He thought back on a few of his partner's words from earlier that week; primarily it was the discussion concerning the stormy weather. The city and surrounding areas had been getting pelted by for over a week and a half.

He remembered how sarcastic he was in the dismissal of the young cadet's remarks, saying to himself, "It's only a storm. It'll eventually blow over." However, now in this perilous moment, he silently acknowledge how his own words had come back to haunt him. John's thoughts shifted back to the present as the vehicle seemed to glide effortlessly on top of the slick grass as it picked up speed during its plunge into the depths of the dark embankment.

Only mere seconds had passed since the whole ordeal began, yet time itself seemed to move in slow motion for the two. Jessie sat in the passenger seat with both of her arms fully extended braced for the inevitable impact that would bring this nightmarish death ride to an end. *Nightmarish* was the correct word fitting for this experience. With every collision of the car's exterior, she could hear her heart pumping in her ears. Each time the car banged against a solid object, both rock and trees alike, she could almost feel the metal bend and contort under the impact as though it were nothing more than plastic shell.

As the front end of the vehicle struck a branch that blocked its path as it raced into the dense vegetation, the lights of the car were shattered. The car was traveling at a rate of forty-five miles an hour when it collided headfirst into a large oak tree. So brutal was the collision that both occupants were rendered unconscious upon impact with the unyielding object.

As fate would have it, no one saw their car swerve in the road and fly over the steep embankment. There would be no team of medical personnel racing up to the scene brandishing life saving equipment with cases of sterilized medicines prepared to render emergency care. All of these things are a luxury, due to their present situation, one that would not be available to John and Jessica Graham.

Save one being who has watched and waited for an opportunity such as this to act, none knew of their perilous condition. Never mind the fact that he was the one responsible for what has just occurred. Mathias' physical form had been shrouded by mist. As always, he fancied himself as an unseen malevolent force, one to not be spied upon by mortal eyes unless he allowed it.

Just as quickly as it began, the rain had miraculously stopped falling, and the rays of the pale moonlight began to pierce the thick canopy of trees, sparsely illuminating the forest below. The light which reflected off the branches seemed to cast eerie shadows on the damp, moss-covered ground below. Mathias began to move closer to the vehicle, and as he did his physical appearance shifted from mist to a more tangible form. Because of the soft, mushy vegetation that surrounded the immediate area, his footfalls were completely silent. However, no tracks were left in his wake; his path would not be visible to any human who would come to this location in the light of day. Once within arm's reach of the passenger-side door, Mathias caught a glimpse of his reflection in the window. Despite his surroundings, he was dressed as immaculately as ever. He wore an expensive business suit of a rich, dark burgundy color, overlaid by a jet-black overcoat, the interior of which was lined with red velvet. Plush fur-lined lapels of grey animal print ran down the length of the garment. Ever so subtle, in two, thin parallel lines, they blended flawlessly into the fabric right beneath the knees.

As he looked at himself in the mirror, he paused momentarily to adjust his tie and play at the diamond cufflinks at his wrist. His hair hung past his shoulders and was being whipped in his face by the cool night breeze. Referring to his long, lustrous, silvery locks, Mathias said to himself beneath his breath, "That will not do at all." He pulled his hair back with both hands and fastened it together with a pendant that materialized from thin air.

"There, that's much better," he said as he ran his hands over the length of his head, smoothing out the locks into a ponytail. His chiseled features, complete with high cheek bones, long narrow nose, and arched brows, shone clearly in the night. Unnatural, emerald-colored eyes looked over his surroundings, especially the reflection of himself, which he came back to for a second time.

He smiled to himself in wicked satisfaction at the craftiness, which had once again delivered that one thing which he coveted most. Mathias peered into the vehicle seeing a battered John Graham slumped over the steering wheel with blood oozing out from a cut over his right eye. Then he looked down at Jessica who sat mere inches away from him. She was still very much unconscious, her head positioned awkwardly with her chin drawn inward against her chest. Despite the superficial wounds she received from the ordeal, he could see the light of her sprit still burning radiantly around her.

Mathias looked down at the door which separated him from his prize. He could see that the metal around the locking mechanism had been damaged from the collision. He ran his hands across the twisted metal until he found a tiny crevice between the door jam. Like a steel vise, he continued to pry his powerful fingers into the gap until he had a firm grip.

After Mathias exerted a small amount of force, the door began to squeal as it gave way and flew off its hinges into the shrubbery. He reached into the wrecked vehicle and pulled Jessica from her seat and carried her away in his arms. As he walked away from the car, he stopped in his tracks and turned around on his heels.

Mathias looked one last time at the man who was trapped in the vehicle, bleeding profusely from his wounds. He showed no trace of emotion as he glanced at John Graham who sat motionless, slumped over the steering wheel. For some time, Mathias stood completely still as if he were reaching out to someone with his thoughts over a great distance. His face was a blank canvas, an emotionless, picturesque model of masculine beauty, almost if he had been cast from marble.

Within moments, a being, clad in all black, appeared out of the shadows and stood directly beside him. Mathias looked over at the immortal that awaited his commands and said, "Finish him off, Drako. And this time leave nothing behind for the one who follows us to recover except for the ashes of his bones!" His silent companion nodded in compliance and watched as Mathias walked past him towards a clearing in the forest. The expression on Mathias face shifted from cold and emotionless to that of a victorious smirk.

Jessie began to stir uneasily as she slowly began to regain consciousness and opened her eyes. Mathias looked down at her, smiling hideously, revealing his fanged teeth. He willed a set of pitch black feathered wings to become visible. They were hideous, yet beautiful all at the same time. Quickly, he unfolded and spread them out to their full length for her to see. These enormous pair of wings extended well above his head. The girl's eyes grew wide as she looked up at him, petrified beyond all reason. Jessie's heart pounded as she attempted to scream, but nothing more than a dry, inaudible rasping sound could be heard.

She recoiled violently and fought hard against him, pounding her fist against his face and chest, trying to escape his grasp. Mathias had no intention of allowing her to slip away from him as he laughed out loud, holding his head back, looking towards the sky. With one fluid motion, he beat his wings hard against the air, and they shot up into the moonlit sky.

Jessie felt as though her heart were going to explode. As she experienced the undeniable sensation of flight, the blood within her veins began to chill, and her stomach churned. Each thrust of his powerful wings took them higher, in a perfect arc. So rapid was their ascent that the wind whipped her hair violently as it stung her face and exposed skin. To avoid passing out, all she could do was to look down towards the dark canopy where she saw her father's car which faded from view as they ascended and disappeared into the clouds.

"Forget him; you belong to me now," Mathias snapped as he looked down at the girl in his arms. Despite the sounds his wings made as they beat forcefully against the wind, she could hear his voice clearly. He pressed her head against his chest, shielding her from the violent wind that carried them. Effortlessly his flight took them on a northwestern course above the clouds.

"In time you shall look back on this moment and come to appreciate this night," Mathias said as he pressed on across the heavens. "I have waited a thousand years for a soul like yours. You have been chosen my child. Tomorrow you shall be reborn into darkness."

Jessica fought desperately to maintain control. As though she had been caught in the eye of a vicious cyclone, her head seemed to swirl around in circles. As consciousness began to slip rapidly away, her vision became blurry. The world around her began to grow dim with each passing moment until darkness inevitably took hold. Every sensation which confirmed her existence and connected her to the mortal plane was stripped away one at time.

It was as if she had been transported to a place where the physical rules which govern humanity were no longer existent. As they disappeared into the clouds, all that was left to her was a conscious mind which was fully aware that Mathias held her captive within his grasp and that she was being carried on wings of death to an unknown destination.

CHAPTER 11

Deadly Encounter

John Graham slowly opened his eyes to find his gaze fixed upon a plate of food that steamed up at him. "Eat up, Honey, your food's getting cold."

A vibrant young woman with long blond hair walked passed him with a child in her arms. She placed the infant in a highchair. John's heart skipped a beat as he looked up with astonishment at the woman who resembled his wife in every way. John shook his head as he attempted to regain his wits.

"I must be dead," John said under his breath as he watched the woman pace from one room to the next gathering childcare articles and placing them in a handbag.

"I've been here before," John thought to himself as he watched his wife walk over towards him and plant a kiss on his lips. Everything about this moment was familiar to him, from the smell of her perfume, to the sounds the wind chimes made as they rattled softly outside the window, pushed by a calm breeze.

He looked down to a newspaper on the table. The date read April 25, 1989. He remembered this day all too well. It was the day that his wife Karen was murdered. He glanced over at her in agony as he watched her feeding their daughter. Every now and then, she would look over at him to say something, but he could not hear her words. It was as if he had been rendered deaf to the sounds of the entire world around him. Nothing penetrated his hearing except the sound the wind chimes made as they rattled in the background.

How many times had he prayed to God that he could relive this moment? There were so many things that John always said that he would have done differently. The first thing would have been to never allow Karen to leave their home that day, even if it meant her losing the job. He would have held her tightly in his arms and begged her to stay home and spend the rest of the day in bed with him. This way he would never have to experience the pain of losing his wife. Agonizing as it was, John could not take his eyes off her. Her navy blue, knee-length skirt and matching blazer fit her slender body perfectly.

This was going to be her first day as a teller at the newly refurbished metropolitan bank. A tear began to well up in John's eyes as he watched the painful scene play itself out. "This is not real," John said as he fought to against his heart. The mist in his mind began to fade away swiftly, and with each passing moment it became clearer that this was nothing more than a fantasy, one which he wanted to exist in but knew he could not. The excruciating pain in his head and bruised rib cage began to intensify as he started to regain consciousness.

John began to remember losing control of the car and their plunge into darkness. The vision of his beloved Karen had all but slipped away from his grasp like water flowing through desperate fingers. More painful than all else was the realism that their moment in time did not exist, and she was nothing more than a fragment of his imagination.

Despite the peril of his situation, he took comfort in this obvious state of delusional bliss. It was almost as if God had really existed and had dispatched angels to him in his time of need to extend a moment's grace. Sweet as it was, John could feel his wife embracing him from behind. Her soft lips pressed lightly against his neck. The smell of her perfume filled his nostrils and seemed to dance in the air around him.

"It's not our time to be together, John," Karen said softly in his ear. "Jessie is going to need you now more than ever. You must go back to her. I will always be with you."

John could feel the delicate grip she had on him loosen, and all the familiar signs of her presence faded away. It was as though a cover was lifted from his eyes. Jonathan Graham awoke to find himself sitting in the wrecked vehicle. Pain shot through his body as he looked out over the steering wheel to see flames beginning to rise from the dented hood. He placed a hand over his swollen left eye and flinched in pain after feeling the huge bruise. The stench of burnt rubber stung his eyes and throat. He looked over for Jessie, only to find an empty seat. Panic raced through him as he attempted to unfasten his seat belt.

He looked over at the gaping hole where the passenger door should have been, and he could tell by the way the metal protruded outward that it had been torn off its hinges by something or someone. His door was barricaded shut by a large oak tree, and the only way out was through the passenger side. The blaze beneath the hood grew more and more intense with each moment. Right before the car exploded, John managed to scramble out of the torched vehicle and crawl on all fours to a safe distance in the clearing. The concussion and heat of the blast took the wind out of him and momentarily illuminated the surrounding area. John lay on the ground for a few seconds trying to recover his strength.

Every ounce of it seemed to have been sapped from his body. Nothing more than his resolve to find his child urged him forward. All the while calling out Jessie's name, he managed to get to his feet and stagger up the path made by the vehicle. The path led back up the hill in a steep incline of forty-five degrees, As he grabbed tree limbs and roots to pull himself up along the trail, John fought through immense levels of pain. He suspected that a couple of his ribs had been either badly bruised or were broken in the accident.

John stopped for a second to catch his breath. It actually hurt for him to breathe. In response to his exertions, John felt the back of his throat and lungs began fill with a warm, salty fluid. It was obvious that he suffered from some internal bleeding. He coughed and winced in agony as he spat out his life's blood on the ground which appeared pitch black in the light of the moon. "Not a good sign at all," John thought to himself as he wheezed painfully to draw the air he desperately needed to survive. After spewing his blood on the ground, he was convinced that he definitely had some internal injuries that needed to be tended to. All of that would have to wait for now; the only thing that mattered was finding Jessie

The further away he climbed from the smoldering wreck, the darker his path became and the more hopeless the task of finding his daughter seemed. There was barely enough light reflected from the wreckage behind him to see his own hands. His heart felt as if it would collapse from the overwhelming feelings of despair which encased and tormented him. John fell to his knees and pounded his fist against the soft earth as he cried Jessie's name aloud into the night. For the first time since he lost his wife, he surrendered completely to the bitter emotions of hopelessness. John covered his face with his palms and bent over in utter defeat. Laying his forehead against the wet ground, silently, without shame, Jonathan Graham wept.

In complete defeat, for minutes he lay prostrate against the ground, weeping uncontrollably at his misfortunes. His mourning was interrupted by the sound of wicked laughter which echoed in the distance. John leapt to his feet and spun around to his left, focusing his gaze towards the direction in which the sound came from.

"Who's out there?" John screamed aloud into the darkness. A few moments passed and there was no response to his call. Only more cruel laughter erupted from the darkness. This time it came from the opposite direction. John turned around again and issued the same question. All the while his emotions shifted from despair to anger. Every fiber of his being told him that whoever it was that tormented him had something to do with Jessie's disappearance.

"Answer me, you son of a bitch!" John screamed out loud into the night air.

The unmistakable sound of a man's voice could be heard clear and distinct through the night. An unnatural mist began to cover the ground at his feet and settle above the branches of the trees until it enveloped him completely. John began to doubt his senses and tried to make a reasonable explanation for the phenomenon his eyes were seeing. He had almost convinced himself that he was still unconscious until he heard the voice again. This time it seemed more potent than before and had an ethereal resonance which penetrated the mist and shadow, causing the hairs on his arms and neck to rise.

John spun around trying to pinpoint the exact location from which the sound originated. His tormentor's laughter could now be heard from all directions. It taunted and terrified him, but most of all it angered him to the depths of his soul. His blood began to boil, stoked by a primal anger he'd never felt before. Instinctively, he bent over and searched the ground for a weapon and found a tree branch large enough for him to wield against any would-be assailant if necessary. John bent his knees slightly and widened his base in preparation for whatever would appear before him through the darkness.

"Ok, you sick bastard, enough of these games. Show yourself!" John said as his face darkened, flushed red with anger. The laughter of the one who taunted him died down and there was a long and empty silence, one which John tried to use to his advantage. He concentrated and focused his hearing and other senses, trying to discern the slightest movement that would give him an indication of where to find his tormentor.

The momentary silence was broken by the demonic entity Drako who began to sing a twisted rendition of a nursery song, one that John must have sung to Jessie at least a thousand times when she was a little girl.

"What kind of twisted game is this?" John said aloud as he narrowed his eyes and strained to see through the mist that surrounded him.

"Little Bo Pete…lost his sheep whose fleece was white as snow. "Now his sheep is gone…poor Pete is all alone... and Death is on his way…"

An eerie resonance flowed behind every syllable; along with it was an unnatural feeling, which lingered in the air.

Suddenly, John was knocked over by a gust of wind as an unseen presence brushed past him and headed down the path leading back towards the wreckage. John got to his feet and heard the sound of feet running swiftly behind him. He spun around and was struck across the face by an invisible claw which left four thin cuts across his left cheek.

John knew without a doubt that he was being toyed with. As thoughts of his daughter's abduction dominated his thoughts, his blood continued to boil with uncontrollable anger. He had already searched the area and there was no trace of her to be found anywhere. Now something lay in wait to finish him off and he was helpless against it.

"How can I possibly hope to fight something I can't see? John thought as he focused on the sounds that surrounded him. Except for the man in the alley a couple of nights ago, he never saw anyone move as fast as this being did. More of the incessant singing and mockery came from the direction of the crash and as John raced back down the hill. Every ounce of his being shook with uncontrollable fury, his entire body ached, and every breath he took brought an indescribable pain upon him.

All of the sensations he felt seemed to fade once he arrived at the burning vehicle and stood in the presence of his aggressor. A figure dressed in all black leather stood a few feet away from the burning vehicle. His back was turned to Jonathan and he continued to hum his wretched tune as he waved his hands playfully across the edge of the flames.

"What did you do with my daughter?" John said as he approached his now silent adversary whose air of defiance pushed him well beyond his limits.

"I asked you a question, God damn it!" John spat as he continued to approach the demon with his feeble weapon in hand, holding it at chest level poised to strike. Drako glanced over his shoulder and forced a smile upon his face, then turned around and continued to move his hands playfully across the flames, his back totally exposed, unmoved by the mortal's acts of aggression towards him.

"Why does it concern you?" She is well beyond your reach now, and her fate now lies in the hands of one who is far greater than you, human." Drako turned around to face his aggressor. His eyes blazed like two red-hot orbs which smoldered like the flames of a blazing inferno. Jonathan's natural reaction caused him to recoil at the sight of the creature that stood before him. Every instinct within told him that whatever it was that stood before him was not human.

"What the hell are you?" John asked as he stepped back.

"I am Drako, one who has been condemned to dwell here among your weak and pathetic kind far longer than you could possibly imagine. Do not trouble yourself about the child. She is no longer your concern. The purpose that she will serve far exceeds your level of understanding.

"As for you, you are mine. I'm going to tear your beating heart from your chest and devour your soul." Drako's eyes narrowed as he gazed at his mortal prey. And in one swift motion, he leapt forward, closing the distance which separated them, lashing out, striking John across the face, sending him flying in the air and crashing against a tree. Totally devastated by the powerful blow, John slumped over in pain. Before he could stand, a foot slammed down on top of his right hand. A wet, snapping sound filled the air as his hand was crushed beneath Drako's boot. John cried out in agony as he rolled over grasping his clawed hand.

Another fist came down across his right shoulder blade causing an unmistakable wet, snapping sound of tendons being torn and bones being broken. John's collar bone was snapped in two beneath the blow. He collapsed from the pain, but his attacker remained relentless and without mercy. He felt a foot kick him violently in the midsection, breaking ribs, and blood gushed uncontrollably from his mouth.

In his painful and near delirious state, many thoughts passed through John's mind. His death was the one thing that stood out more than all others. He always remembered hearing the tales of individuals who had near-death experiences and lived to tell of it, particularly those who said that in the final moments of life right before death they had experienced an overwhelming feeling of peace and contentment. Some people claimed to have seen their entire life flash before their eyes. One happy moment right after the next, no pain, no feelings of sorrow, only bliss.

"Total bullshit! That must have been heaven for them, but my experience is less than peachy. Here I'm getting the holy hell beat out of me by something that's definitely not classified as human," John thought as he tried to defend himself against the brutal onslaught.

How nice it would have been to have led a long, prosperous life into a ripe old age, one which allowed him an opportunity of seeing his daughter grow into womanhood. Or to pass away on his deathbed comforted by memories of how on her wedding day he gave her away to a young man whom he approved of.

It would be nice to die a natural death knowing that he had grandchildren or even great grandchildren to continue his legacy. If his end was one filled with sweet memories such as these, then death would have been accepted with open arms. Unfortunately, this was not the case. The only thing that John felt was pain, combined with an overwhelming sense of emptiness. There were no pleasant fantasies of his growing old surrounded by his grandchildren to ease his passing. As John began to drift into darkness, he began to hallucinate as he saw an image of his daughter's face appear right before his eyes.

He managed to sit upright and placed his back against a tree for additional support. In his deluded state, he reached out with one hand toward the vision, attempting to touch his daughter's face one last time. His heart wrenched in agony as the vision faded and the real world became more vivid as ever. Drako loomed over him like a specter of death, his jewel studded dagger in hand poised and ready for the kill. Due to a spinal injury he suffered at the hands of his demonic adversary, John was absolutely helpless. With each second that passed, he could feel his limbs begin to tingle and grow numb as partial paralysis set in. He felt himself beginning to lose consciousness again, slowly passing into darkness as his labored breathing and pulse slowed to a faint and near undetectable rhythm.

"I'm sorry that I failed you, Jessie," John said as he readied himself for the finishing blow. Drako had drawn his razor sharp dagger back prepared to deal the death blow when his eyes grew wide with astonishment and a gurgling sound escaped his throat. An invisible hand held him fast within a vise like grip, and slowly lifted him until his feet dangled six inches off the ground. Drako began to wince and writhe in pain, struggling violently to free himself. Back and forward, he kicked his legs, thrashing about like a trout caught in a fisherman's net.

The more he struggled, the tighter the grip on him became until he could no longer hold his weapon. Eventually he let it go and pried with both hands at his neck, attempting to free himself. His eyes were now strained to the point as if they were going to pop out of their sockets. John could see an image becoming visible as it carried the flailing demon away from him. It was the man he had encountered in the alley a few days prior. John had fought to maintain consciousness but was jolted when he saw the set of wings which were draped behind the man's back. Raziel tossed his captive across the clearing with one hand, and in one fluid motion, he drew his sword.

His ethereal weapon blazed white-hot and gave off the purest light, one which John had never seen before. So intense was this light that he had to turn his head and shield his eyes as it repelled all the darkness that surrounded them. Trying to fend off the light, Drako raised his dagger. He recoiled in terror at the mere sight of the being who stood before him. In search of refuge, instinctively he turned towards the deepening shadows, desperately searching the trees, seeking a sure route to escape his eradication. His movements were so swift it gave the illusion of teleportation. It was as though he would disappear from one spot only to reappear in another. Though he moved with blinding speed, it was not fast enough to escape his fate.

Before Drako could take flight, Raziel blocked the retreat of his cowardly adversary and plunged his sword straight through the demon's chest. The impelled demon let out a deafening, high-pitched shriek of agony before erupting into flames and began to disintegrate right before John's eyes. Raziel stood motionless over the spot where the final remains of his enemy burned and smoldered until it was reduced to nothing more than a pile of ash. He looked down and retrieved the dagger which had embedded itself in the earth.

"Such is the fate of those who are counted among the fallen," Raziel said as he turned and walked towards John Graham who lay slumped over near death. Raziel had swiftly crossed the distance that separated him and the wounded man. Slowly, he kneeled down and placed an outstretched hand upon John's broken body. Raziel closed his eyes and drew in a deep breath; he concentrated for a moment and channeled his powers of healing into the mortal.

"It's not too late for this one," Raziel said as he looked up towards the sky. A cool breeze swept a few strands of hair into his face as he lowered his head and continued to focus his energies. Just by the subtle changes in the air, he knew that dawn was upon them. The clouds just above the horizon began to shift to lighter shades of red and burgundy in the twilight. Raziel's powers seemed to increase with the rising of the sun, his body shifted from solid to a more translucent ethereal form.

He began to emit a faint light that pulsated and grew into a blue aura that surrounded his angelic form. He willed his energy to pass from him and envelope the man who lay helplessly beneath him. Slowly, he poured his essence over the wounded man who instantly began to heal. Within seconds, the cuts on his face that bled profusely, sealed themselves. The bruise that had caused his left eye to be closed fell away and was no more. As the angelic power flowed through him, his broken fingers began to mend and correct themselves.

John was barely conscious but could feel his body tingle as his mangled form was slowly beginning to mend under the touch of the stranger who had saved him from certain death. Slowly, he opened his eyes and gasped in terror at the sight of the translucent being of light that kneeled over him.

Raziel looked down at the man, smiled, and said, "Be still. You have nothing to fear from me, or the one who attacked you. He is no longer among us.

"What are you?" John said as he attempted to stand to his feet. Raziel gently placed a hand on his shoulder and settled him back down. "You are no longer in danger. Your wounds will be healed momentarily. As for what I am, we both know that you would not accept the answer that I would give. I've looked into your soul once before. Although you are a good man, you are in danger of being lost because of your lack of faith and the guilt that you carry within."

"What the hell are you talking about?" John said as he stood to his feet. Raziel paused as though he were measuring his words before giving an answer. "You continue to torment yourself for your wife's death and blame God for your misfortunes. Although He presides over us all, He is not the cause of these tragedies. There are forces which oppose him, attempting to overthrow the balance which he established at the dawn of time. I know that your child has been taken. The connection that exists between you and the child enables me to sense her presence in this world. She is alive, but for how long I cannot be sure."

Raziel walked over to the clearing in the forest where Mathias once stood holding his captive. He closed his eyes and focused his supernatural senses, pushing them to limits that far exceeded any detection device made by man. It wasn't long before he was able to locate a faint trace of his quarry on the wind.

"The connection between you and your daughter is strong," Raziel said. "However, I will need your aid if we hope to find her in time."

"Why is this happening to us?" John said as he stood beside the angelic warrior who towered above him.

"All of the things that are happening now have already been foretold. Your child has been chosen to serve as the portal for those who have fallen to pass into this realm. If they are allowed to cross over into the mortal plane, they will bring a level of death and destruction that is far beyond mortal reckoning." Raziel paced back and forth as though he was focusing on something that hung in the air. It was intangible and undetectable to all save him. "The presence that lingers here is one that I have sensed before," Raziel said as he gritted his teeth.

"*Mathias!*" There was rage in his tone as he spoke the name of the powerful immortal who had fought many battles at his side during ancient times. Vivid pictures of Mathias' betrayal burned deeply within his mind. Raziel reflected back to the day when the tides shifted against him, and his companion fell prey to lust and the promise of power.

"So you know who is responsible for all of this?" John said as he edged closer towards the furious being who pulsated with energy.

"Yes, I know the one who is responsible for these despicable acts. He is my brother. For centuries I have tracked him across the face of the earth. He now serves the Dark Lord who would see this world burn. Until now, Mathias had been successful in eluding me, masking his presence behind his evil companion." Raziel glanced over at the smoldering pile of demonic ashes.

"Mathias doesn't realize the error he made in taking your child and leaving you behind for dead," Raziel said, extending a hand outwards. "Take hold and do not fear. We must make haste if we are to save her." Reluctantly, John reached out and took hold of the massive hand that beckoned him. Instantly, there was a blinding flash of light, and as the two figures vanished without a trace, the spot where they stood was now empty. One bound by an eternal oath to confront an ancient adversary, the other caught in the middle of a battle that may claim his life or forfeit the soul of his beloved child.

To Be Continued

Book II
Nemesis
Dark Apprentice

Printed in the United States
62641LVS00002B/19

9 781598 002447